GRINGO GOLD

GRINGO GOLD

Savi   , Matt Sullivan in the Amarillo Desert
led   Clint Bellamy and Max Juarez to
help   g a wagon-train that had attracted
thie   s and killers like a magnet. The gold
cros   he immigrants carried was the lure
that   ought violence at every twist of the
trail   reed drove men to deeds of mayhem
and   uplicity as they vied to possess the
cros   and desirable Kathy Mullins caused
comp cations for the pards. Her lover,
Mat   vas charged with murder in Portales,
and   ooked set to hang. Even Kathy believed
him   ilty.

GRINGO GOLD

by

Hal Jons

The Golden West Large Print Books
Long Preston, North Yorkshire,
BD23 4ND, England.

British Library Cataloguing in Publication Data.

Jons, Hal
    Gringo gold.

      A catalogue record of this book is
      available from the British Library

      ISBN   978-1-84262-887-4 pbk

First published in Great Britain in 1981 by Robert Hale Ltd.

Published in Large Print 2015 by arrangement with
Hal Jons, care of Mrs M. Kneller

The Golden West Large Print is an imprint of Library Magna
Books Ltd.

Printed and bound in Great Britain by
T.J. (International) Ltd., Cornwall, PL28 8RW

CHAPTER ONE

The last swirling dust particles swept away to the north revealing the two alkali-covered men leading horses unrecognizable as a pinto and dun gelding. The dust storm had lasted a full day and night. When it was apparent that the storm centre had shifted, the men removed the protective bandannas from their faces and stared at each other out of painful eyes. The shorter man tried to clear his throat and gave it up. Instead he unfastened his canteen and gargled carefully. He handed the canteen to his companion who grinned his appreciation, showing even white teeth that gleamed in contrast to the overall covering of grey.

'Reckoned we were stuck in that storm for keeps, Mex,' the stockier man grunted.

'Sure was a humdinger,' replied Mex Juarez.

They dusted themselves down then stripped the gear from their horses, brushing every vestige of dust from the animals' coats revealing the natural colouration of the pinto stallion and dun gelding. With equal care they brushed the particles out of saddlery and gear before refastening everything in place. Using their hats they poured a measure of water out of a skin water-jack for each animal and controlled the intake carefully.

The sun escaped from the dust pall and its searing rays glared down on the desert with pitiless intensity. Thankfully the pards climbed into their saddles and set their mounts moving. The Mexican lit up a cheroot whilst Clint Bellamy, the Texan, rolled himself a thicker than usual cigarette by way of celebration.

They saw the low-flying vultures at the same time, and the prone figure beside a heavily built horse. They gigged their horses into a run, sending the vultures up high into the brassy sky. As the pards dropped to the ground they saw the man was no wandering cowhand. He was dressed in a plaid flannel shirt, corduroy trousers, hobnailed ankle boots, a neckerchief tied in a tight roll, and beside him was a headpiece that was favoured by the new immigrants from Ireland. The horse, drooping in a state of dehydration, had no saddle, just a blanket draped over its back and a length of rope joined both ends of the bit in its mouth.

As Clint turned the man over, Mex handed down his canteen so that a few drops could be trickled into the man's mouth. There was a gash just above the left temple and blood and dust made it look a coagulated mess, but Clint decided it was not serious. At the scent

8

of water the big draught horse lumbered forward and Mex used his hat to slake its thirst.

It took a few minutes for the precious liquid to have an effect on the man but at length his eyelids fluttered and he stirred in Clint's arms. The Texan cleaned the clogging alkali from the man's face and bathed the wound then suddenly the eyes opened and he stared up at Clint uncomprehendingly. The Texan stood up and waited for him to gather his wits. They could now see that he was no more than seventeen or eighteen years of age. The eyes were as green as the lush grass of South Carolina and the shock of tightly curling hair as red as a Montana sunset.

'Bejabers, what hit me?' the youngster asked in a strange accent. 'And where am I?' he struggled to get to his feet and the pards lent helping hands until he stood four-square on size thirteen feet, a gaunt, gangling figure showing promise of attaining giant proportions in fullness of time.

'Save the talking,' said Mex. 'We'll get you on to that cayuse and get the hades out of this sun bowl.'

The Mexican handed the youngster his strange-shaped hat and the pards heaved him astride the draught horse, then they mounted and headed south. After a couple more libations of water from Mex's canteen the youngster was sufficiently recovered to talk freely. He told them his name was Matt Sullivan and they listened to his story with mounting interest.

'My moniker's Bellamy, Clint Bellamy, and my pard's Mex Juarez,' the Texan said, turning in his saddle to study the young greenhorn. 'How come you're parted from your folk and stuck in the middle of nowhere without a saddle-roll?'

'I was looking for the Holy Father...' Sullivan started, then seeing the pards' nonplussed expressions tried again. 'Maybe I'd better start from the beginning.' The pards nodded so he continued. 'About five months ago all the folk living in our village, that is Mournaghee in Southern Ireland, set off for America in Captain Moriarty's ship the *Northern Light*. For a couple of years the potato crop had failed and the way the captain talked of America, he persuaded folk that they'd make a better life in the New Country. Anyway we landed at Norfolk about three months ago.'

'So you all joined a wagon train?' Mex asked.

'Well, we didn't join up with anyone else,' Sullivan answered. 'We'd brought our own wagons and horses but we'd have had to go along with other settlers if it hadn't been for meeting up with a wagon boss called Ross Dorgan who said he'd take us to California.'

'So Dorgan took charge, eh?' Clint put in.

'That's right. He had two scouts called Abe Ringo and Jim Lee and his cook was a Swede named Sven Borg.' The youngster paused, sorting things out into the right order. 'And just before we left Norfolk a priest named Father Dewar joined us. Most of my folk take their religion seriously so they were all pleased to have the holy father along. He took care of the money and of course the cross.'

'What cross?' Mex asked, more out of politeness than interest.

'The one we brought from Mournaghee,' the youngster replied. 'It's about this big.' He spread his arms to indicate about three feet one way and two feet the other. 'Solid gold, with a big ruby where the arms join the upright and around the ruby it has three rings of diamonds.'

The pards whistled their amazement.

'Life couldn't have been that bad if your folk could afford to buy a cross like that,' commented Mex.

'Oh we didn't buy it, mister,' Sullivan replied quickly. 'The story goes that a Spanish ship was driven off course and piled up on the rocks below the village and the cross was salvaged. That was close on a couple of hundred years ago, and the cross had been in the village church ever since.'

'This Dorgan,' Clint said. 'Did he know you had the cross before he became your

11

wagon boss?'

'I don't know. We were kept in the bay a week at Norfolk before landing but some of the crew went ashore. They could have talked about it. Mind, Mister Dorgan and his men were mighty good.'

'Were?' Mex said. 'What happened to them then?'

'Well a few days ago some riders joined up with us. The boss man called himself Gabe Dance. They were good enough company for a while then they started picking quarrels with the wagon boss and his men. There was a lot of shooting and Mister Dorgan, Ringo and Borg were killed. The other man, Jim Lee, got away. Dance and his men said they'd lead us to Santa Fe then a couple of days ago they led the wagon train into a canyon that narrowed to just a bit more than wagon width and petered out into a blind end. Well they struck down Father Dewar, stole the cross and most of our money, and when Mike Milligan and Rory Mullins tried to stop them Dance shot them both dead.'

'So they left you stuck in the canyon?' Clint asked.

Sullivan nodded. 'That's right. We spent the rest of the day and night searching for water but we didn't find any, and considering we hadn't stocked up for a week things were getting desperate. Then next morning the holy father rode out. He wanted to pray alone for our safety and the return of the cross. Well a long time went by and he didn't come back so I set out to look for him. After riding for an hour or so I saw some riders ahead just rounding the line of hills. I went after them, thinking the priest might have got into trouble with Dance but they seemed to disappear into the hillside. Sometime later I came to the gap that opens out into this desert land. I know I should have turned back but whenever the haze cleared I could see riders, so I kept on. When they started shooting I was going to turn back but one of the bullets grazed my head and I was nearly unconscious for a while. Then the dust storm started and the last I remember was falling off my horse.'

'You sure ran into a rough time feller,' was Mex's comment. 'So the whole wagon train is stuck in the middle of nowhere without a single *hombre* who knows the territory?' Mex went on. The youngster's expression was woebegone.

'Yes sir,' he replied. 'There's a lot of good folk going to die unless they get help, and they deserve better.'

'I reckon you're right,' said Clint Bellamy. 'Mex and me have nothing special on hand right now, we might be able to help.'

A light came into the youngster's green eyes. 'You'll make yourselves a lot of friends if you do,' he said with simple dignity.

13

The hills showed up in the distance, clearing the haze. The sand became interspersed with sparse shrub that grew thicker with every mile they rode, until they came to where the hills closed in and funnelled through to the plains beyond, and now they rode with parched bunch-grass beneath their horses' hooves. When they emerged on to the plain with the outer slopes of the hills rolling to the north-west and north-east they drew rein. Clint and Mex swivelled in their saddles and looked to the youngster for guidance. He pointed to the north-east.

'That's the way I came,' he said, and satisfied, the pards gigged their mounts forward.

They rode along the foot of the hills for about four miles, then the quest was over. A few miles away the immigrants were assisting themselves. A ring of wagons were huddled near to the base of the hill and as the three men approached they saw another wagon roll out of the canyon, drawn out backwards by a team of six horses.

A knot of people stood outside the ring of wagons watching the approach of Matt Sullivan and the pards and calling to kinsfolk and gesticulating excitedly. By the time Matt Sullivan rode into their midst and the pards drew rein twenty yards or so away, about half-a-dozen gaunt, shirt-sleeved men fronted the group, each holding a scattergun. They all looked grim enough to use them before asking questions. Behind them the womenfolk, dusty, unwashed, but for the most part attractive, gazed stony-faced at the newcomers.

Matt Sullivan dismounted and pushed his way back to the front of the group.

'These men are my friends,' he remarked to the central figure, a big, dark-visaged man. 'They saved me when I was lost in the sand storm and brought me back.'

'And who did that to you?' the man asked in a brogue that set Mex and Clint grinning despite themselves.

Matt Sullivan's hand went up involuntarily to the wound on his temple. 'I was fired on by some riders before the dust storm started.'

'And how do you know it wasn't these riders?'

'I just know,' the youngster replied. 'The men who fired at me were the ones who took the cross.'

The big fellow still looked doubtful. 'What are you planning to do?' he asked the pards.

'We figured you could use some help considering there's nobody who knows the territory.' It was the Texan who spoke.

'And why do you want to help?' The big fellow's face was grim. 'There's nothing left to steal.'

Matt Sullivan spread his hands and looked apologetically at the two men who had rescued him. They ignored the man's remark.

'I guess you've got cause to be bitter,' Clint said quietly. 'And it'll mebbe take you a long time to sort out who you can trust. The point is though, you're short on water and lost in the middle of nowhere so you'd better make up your mind right now whether you want us along or not.'

The leader lowered his scattergun and the other men followed his lead. 'We've no choice, stranger,' he replied. 'As you said, we're lost and likely to die of thirst before another day is through. If you mean to help then we're going to be thanking you for the rest of our days.'

Clint Bellamy nodded and his face split into the grin that transformed his weather-beaten features into handsome lines. 'I guess we'll get along fine,' he said. 'My moniker is Clint Bellamy an' my pard is Mex Juarez.'

The big fellow strode forward and looked up into both men's faces before the hardness of his features relaxed. 'Rory Clancy is my name.' He swept his arm around, indicating the other men who still stood behind him. 'And there's O'Flaherty, O'Reilly, Matthews, Reardon, Kelly, Maloney and O'Callaghan.'

Bellamy and Juarez raised their hands in acknowledgement and the Irishmen raised their quaint bowler hats in return. Another wagon came backwards out of the blind canyon, the team of six sorry-looking horses being rushed by a few more men dressed in the same garb as the other immigrants, bowler hat, knotted kerchief, thick flannel collarless shirt, corduroy trousers tied just below the knee and heavy ankle boots. These men got the wagon into its place and un-hitching the team, started towards the group of men and women standing behind Clancy. He whirled around on them, his face black as thunder.

'Get on with it, McTigue!' he yelled. 'You've got four more to drag out.'

McTigue stopped, then with a grin and a shrug of his big shoulders turned around sending the other men scuttling for the canyon mouth. He followed, leading the weary team. The pards noticed all the other horses that were dotted around were in no better shape. They needed water, and soon.

Children stared down at the pards from the wagons and from the look of them, they at least had not yet gone short of water. Clint tightened his belt a notch. There was work to do before he could allow himself a meal. Mex climbed out of the saddle and unhitched the skin water-carriers from both mounts. He poured a small measure into his hat for the pinto and dun gelding then he handed the carriers over to Clancy. The big Irishman's face creased into a smile, and pushing his way through the group of men, handed the water containers to a tall buxom woman.

'Share that out where it's wanted most, Kate,' he said, and the woman flashed a grateful look towards the pardners before moving away.

'If you'll get your water wagons hitched up, Clancy you'll have all the water you want five hours from now,' Clint called out. 'I believe the Little Amarillo is no more than eight miles north.'

Clancy barked orders and men rounded up two teams of horses and while Clint rolled himself a smoke they hitched the animals to the big open-topped wagons. Mex led his horse to where the bunch grass grew greenest and ground hitched it. He carried his gear to the ring of boxes set around the cook's fire. When the water wagons rolled out in Bellamy's wake Mex was surrounded by curious children and a ring of grown-ups, all eager to hear that he and his pardner would be able to see them safely to their destination.

The loss of the cross seemed to have drained away a lot of the optimism which they must have held at the start of their long trek, and Mex reckoned they would have to be much closer to California before they would laugh heartily again.

Curtis the cook, handed a bowl to the Mexican with about two inches of stew in the bottom and Mex took it with the gravity and grace of a man receiving an invitation to join a banquet. He nodded his appreciation to Curtis and turned his attention to Rory Clancy. 'How long have you been on the trail?' he asked.

'Come daylight tomorrow makes three months,' Clancy replied, sitting beside him.

'Did Dorgan tell you which trail he was taking before he got killed?'

Clancy nodded. 'He was making for Santa Fe, then on through Colorado into Utah to cross the mountains, and back south-west into Nevada, through the Mojave Desert and across the Sierra Nevadas to the coast.'

Mex lit up a cheroot and considered things before replying. 'It's likely Dorgan knew what he was doing,' he said at length. 'And no doubt he'd have seen you through, but I can't help thinking you'd run plumb into trouble crossing the mountains at the peak of the trail in Utah and again crossing the Mojave Desert.'

Clancy's face was serious as Mex talked on and the faces of the other immigrants mirrored their leader's concern.

'I guess the best route now is south to Big Springs and the Gila trail. The going's tough but possible any time of the year. About eighty days would see you wherever you aim on settling.'

'We've got three months behind us so I'm thinking another eighty days won't kill us,' remarked Clancy.

'All you've done up to now is cross the

plains,' Mex said soberly. 'Which ever route you take from here it's gonna be nothing but mountains, rivers and deserts.'

The light of determination came into Clancy's eyes.

'Mountains, rivers and deserts are there to be crossed, mister,' he said decisively and a growl of approval came from his followers.

The Mexican grinned and drew on his cheroot. 'Sure you'll cross 'em but you'll have to travel light and faster than you've managed as yet.'

'We'd travel a lot better if we had the old Spanish cross back in its place.' It was the big, buxom woman who had shared out the water who spoke, and the others nodded.

Mex stood up and stared at the immigrants with a degree of impatience. 'That cross isn't going to drag you over the mountains and haul you through dust and sand axle high, and turn into water when you're dying of thirst. There's only one thing that's gonna get you through to where you're heading, and that's spunk!'

The Irish looked unimpressed. Their faith went deep.

'You've got a choice,' Mex went on. 'Either my pard and me will go chase the *hombres* who stole your cross, in which case you stay and roast right here, or we'll guide you clear to Pasadena. What's it to be?'

'The cross didn't bring much luck to the

Spaniards who sailed in the *Santa Barbara*.' Young Matt Sullivan pushed his way to the front as he spoke. 'I think we should take up Mister Juarez' offer to guide us.'

'Seems to me that's good sense, Matt,' replied Clancy. 'If there was any luck in that cross we wouldn't be here right now.'

The words must have sounded like heresy to the listeners but their present plight tempered their religious instincts, and in groups they moved away to their wagons.

'Now that's settled,' Mex said, 'we'd better check on the wagons and throw away any surplus gear.'

The two men went from wagon to wagon inspecting bodywork, wheels and axles for flaws, and Mex was agreeably surprised at the sturdy construction of the wagons. The big draught horses were in poorer state, being unused to the dry bunch-grass that covered the Texan Plains. He reckoned they would need a lot of nursing when the going got tougher but once arrived in California they would settle in all right.

Any suggestion by Mex that a family should dispense with a bulky item of furniture was stonily refused, and at the end of his tour he had been unable to lighten the load one iota. 'Next time I tell 'em they'll do as I say,' he said quietly. 'By that time they'll have seen sense.'

Clancy did not answer. He was acutely conscious that the still, taking up a third of his wagon space should be jettisoned first of all, but he'd get that damned still to California if he had to carry it himself.

The sun was beating down with torrid strength and people were crawling under their wagons to shelter from its rays. Mex leaned back against the blistering paintwork of Clancy's wagon and smoked contentedly. The Irishman, wiping the streaming perspiration from his face regarded the Mexican with some respect.

'You look like the heat doesn't bother you, mister,' he said, casting longing eyes on the space underneath his wagon.

Mex grinned. 'Sure, heat bothers me same as most folk, I guess you'll see that for yourself when we get down along the Gila.'

'You mean it's going to be hotter than this?'

'Yeah. A whole heap hotter.'

Clancy groaned and with a hurried excuse, crawled under the wagon. Mex was the only one awake in the camp, and marvelling at the naivety of the immigrants not posting guards, when the dust clouds in the distance told him that Clint was bringing the water wagons in.

CHAPTER TWO

The rumbling of the wagons and the shouting of the drovers aroused the sleeping Irish folk, and conscious again of the thirst that enervated them, they struggled to their feet and rushed to meet the wagons. Mex stayed put. He was more interested in the dozen riders flanking Clint. Only when he saw the Texan's guns in their holsters did he relax.

The riders dismounted in the centre of the ring of wagons whilst the settlers surrounded the water-wagons, badgering the drovers to satisfy their immediate needs.

Four of the horsemen followed Bellamy as he strolled across to meet Mex. The others stood eyeing the Irish with a complete lack of interest. Mex nodded to the Texan whilst appraising the other men. One of them, a stocky oldster dressed in buckskin, wore a sheriff's badge.

'My sidekick, Mex Juarez,' Clint said. 'This is Jim Lee, Luke Vane, Sheriff of Amarillo, Dan Salter and Ike Webber.'

The men nodded briefly and Mex's attention turned on Jim Lee. He was a tall spare man with good features and serious grey eyes. 'You the Jim Lee that was scouting for this wagon train?' Mex asked.

'Yeah the same,' Lee replied. 'There was nothing I could do at the time. I was riding in when I saw my sidekicks go under.' The man's features were under control but the pards could tell the death of Dorgan, Ringo and Borg had affected him deeply. 'I reckoned I'd do more good getting help than horning in and getting killed.'

Some of the settlers drew attention to his return. He was soon surrounded by a crowd who were obviously pleased to see him back. Rory Clancy pushed his way to the front and clasped Lee like a long lost brother. Luke Vane turned his back on the proceedings and took stock of Clint and Mex.

'You *hombres* see any sign of Dance when crossing the Amarillo Strip?'

'Nope, not a trace,' Mex replied. 'I guess we kept pretty close to the shortest route even though we hit a mighty thick dust storm, but mebbe Dance travelled wide, or mebbe headed into the Strip as a blind.'

'Could be,' Vane replied tersely. His expression implied that he would form his own opinions. 'Wa'al, it looks like the wagon train can look after itself now that Lee has taken on Salter and Webber. I'll head that posse after Gabe Dance.'

'You heard of Dance before?' asked Clint.

'Yeah, sure thing. He shot up an escort taking Mose Belman into Fort Munro for hang-

24

ing, then held up a couple of Wells Fargo stages between the Casa Grande and Tucson. That was a year ago. Most folk reckoned the gang had split up an' gone east.'

Vane pushed through the crowd to where his posse waited. Clint and Mex followed and watched the men swing astride their mounts. There was nothing in the appearance of the sworn-in deputies to inspire confidence, and the quick exchange of glances when Vane growled his intentions, suggested to the pards that the deputies were about their own business and in no way concerned with law and order.

The sheriff rode off but his deputies took their time. One of them, a big, bleak-faced man astride a jet-black stallion, leaned over and tapped Matt Sullivan on the shoulder. 'That right the cross was solid gold, feller?'

The youngster nodded. 'Yes, it's solid gold through and through, with a big ruby and rings of diamonds in it.' He stretched out his arms to indicate the size, and with a grin the deputy rode away, followed closely by the others. Clint and Mex exchanged significant glances.

Jim Lee started in right away to organize the wagon train ready for moving, and already the water-wagons were being driven into the central position to allow people to draw their supplies. 'Tell 'em to get a meal under their belts quickly,' he was saying to

Clancy when the pards joined him. 'We'll see sundown at a water-hole on the Bar K.'

'And what about Father Dewar?' Clancy demanded. 'Are we to go on without trying to find him?'

Lee nodded. 'Seems he's been long enough gone to be past help. I guess you've just gotta accept he's dead. Anyways we've gotta get moving. Salter and Webber have got just three months before they're due on a cattle drive. We aim to get you to California with time to spare.'

'Which way are you heading?' Mex asked as Clancy went off shouting orders.

'Only way I know,' Lee replied. 'It's down to Big Springs and Odessa for me, then over the Pecos and Rio Grande for the Gila Trail.'

'That's sure enough the best trail,' Mex agreed, then as a thought struck him. 'Those deputies of Vane's, are they his regular deputies.'

Jim Lee shrugged his slim shoulders. His concern was purely for the wagon train. 'I reckon not. His regular men were riding the section when I showed up. He swore in that bunch in a drinking parlour. I guess they were just riding through.'

'That's what I figured,' Mex replied with a grimace.

'One thing's sure,' Jim Lee gritted. 'When I've done leading this wagon train to California, I aim to catch up with the *hombres* that gunned down my sidekicks if they get clear of Vane, if it takes me a lifetime.'

'I sure appreciate the way you feel,' Clint put in. 'Now that you're gonna head the wagon train I guess me an' my pard could try trailing the killers.'

Jim Lee's steady eyes rested a long time on the two men. 'If I didn't take you for a pair of straight-shooters I'd say you just wanted to get your fingers on that cross. As it is I guess you've got your own reasons for tangling with that bunch of murderers. Are you lawmen?'

Clint and Mex shook their heads.

'We've just got time to kill,' Mex said easily.

Jim Lee nodded and strode away to check on the preparations for a meal. A girl with a mass of dark, wavy hair came away from the shelter of the wagons and slipped into step beside him, her face turned animatedly towards the scout.

'I guess we know why he's so all-fired keen to see the wagon train safely on its way,' Clint remarked dryly and the Mexican's teeth showed in a wide grin.

'Always there's a woman,' Mex said. 'A man is always running to or away from a woman.'

Clint considered his pard with mock seriousness. 'Y'know, Mex, I still haven't figured just which of those two things you're doing.'

The Mexican's eyebrows went up. 'Me – I

reckon I run from all women.'

The pards joined in the meal prepared by Matt Sullivan's mother, whose gratitude for having brought the youngster back safely was in every glance, and the young giant of an Irishman showed he set some store on all the pards said. There was genuine disappointment when Clint told them he and Mex would be riding on, but when he said the intention was to catch up with Gabe Dance and return the cross, both Matt and his mother nodded their appreciation.

The meal was eaten and Jim Lee got the wagon train sorted out in order, then with Salter riding on well ahead and Webber at the rear, he rode the line as the wagons rumbled and creaked over the rough, uneven ground. Clint and Mex rode wide of the wagons to escape the dust that rose in a heavy pall. They reckoned on taking another meal at the waterhole ahead, then skirting the hills south of the Amarillo Strip, to seek out any sign that might lead them to Dance.

Hours slipped away as the lumbering wagons seemed to inch their way across the wilderness of sparse bunch-grass. Hours when the sun sucked the fire and life out of beasts and humans, hours when the sore-eyed men hunched up on the driving seats of their wagons, conjured up dreams of the lush meadows of the land they had left behind. Many a mouth was twisted with the bitterness of disappointment, and many doubted the wisdom behind this search for a new way of life.

CHAPTER THREE

needed half an hour to sundown when
e ordered the wagon train to take up
ght formation beneath the steep walls of
e Little Pueblo Mountains, the range that
closed the Amarillo Desert. When the
gons were turned inwards in a neat circle,
int Bellamy and Mex Juarez packed away
e supply of hard rations Lee handed out
d after waving a farewell to the crowd of
en and women encircling the hastily
ected field kitchen, climbed into their
ddles and rode into the night.

amie Reardon turned to Mike Kelly, with
t, suspicious eyes alight. 'I'm betting those
o are smart enough to catch up with the
lers who stole the cross,' he said. 'And
ep it too,' he added.

Mike Kelly nodded his big bull head. 'I
ouldn't blame 'em,' he replied. 'If I could
t hold of it I'd keep it myself.'

Now you're talking,' Reardon became
imated. 'If we keep close to those two
hat's to stop us taking the cross from 'em?'

Kelly's expression was doubtful. 'We
uldn't keep 'em in sight on our horses,
nie and the country's a bit too rugged for

31

my fancy.'

Neither man noticed Matt Sullivan behind them.

'We'll travel fast an' catch up with 'em,' said Reardon. 'Persuade 'em we want to tag along an' help. I'm betting they won't waste time turning back.'

Agreement passed between them and without further ado they ransacked the wagon their shared for blankets, saddles and saddlebags, then to the surprise of everyone they announced their intention to help Bellamy and Juarez to recover the cross. Jim Lee expressed himself in the forthright manner of a man well qualified to give an opinion.

'What help do you *hombres* think you can give to those two? All you're gonna do if you ever catch up with 'em is hold 'em back. You need years in this country before you can look after yourselves, leave alone help anyone.'

Jamie Reardon held up his rifle. 'I can take the middle out of a can at five hundred yards with this, mister. No one's got to nurse Jamie Reardon.'

Jim Lee turned away with a shrug. It was nothing to do with him if some of the immigrants chose to throw away their lives. Reardon and Kelly rode away in silence. There was a lot of head shaking amongst the men and some spiteful looks amongst the single females. Whereas Reardon nor Kelly had never moved out of their ways to help anyone before, their present action set the men thinking; the two were unmarried and even their temporary loss to the community was of some concern to the women. When Matt Sullivan prepared to follow the two men ten minutes later however there was a clamour from all quarters as folk persuaded him to stay. The noise increased when Kathy Mullins joined him astride a big, deep-chested Suffolk. His mother stared at him wide-eyed, willing him not to go, but Matt's mind was made up. He owed his life to the two pardners and after overhearing Reardon and Kelly plotting together he reckoned he had a chance to square things.

Jim Lee turned to Rory Clancy who stood scratching his head in bewilderment as the fading light closed in on the last two riders to leave camp.

'There's sure gonna be some mayhem on account of that cross you toted from your home country,' he said quietly. 'I guess Dance an' his gang are all ready to kill each other for it by now, then there's Luke Vane headin' a posse of hard-lookers trailing 'em close, and Bellamy, Juarez an' your folk.' He looked hard at Clancy whose face was troubled. 'If ever you see it back I'd get it melted down pronto an' shared out. I'd say a wooden cross would serve you better.'

'How much longer are we gonna stay in this hole?'

The speaker, Gabe Dance, a big, hard-faced man, stared out of unwinking eyes at the tall slim man who stood watching four others playing at a card game with a dog-eared set of cards. The card players shot glances up at the boss, waiting for his answer.

'A couple more days I guess,' Mose Belman replied. 'If you *hombres* had killed Lee we could have travelled straight on. Maybe he saved his skin and kept going but I don't reckon so. What I saw of Lee tells me he'd travel fast to the nearest town and stir up the law, then rustle up help for those damned settlers.'

Gabe Dance shrugged angrily. 'So he gets help, that makes it more sensible to keep moving fast.'

There was a growl of approval from the card players but Belman shook his head, and when he looked at Dance his eyes snapped fire.

'That way we're on the run, never knowing who's on our trail. I picked Rimrock because there's no other way into it except the road that climbs up from each side of the valley. If there's anyone tailing us I want 'em to catch up right here, and when we go on we can leave 'em buried right here.'

Gabe Dance snorted. He had been too long without hard liquor for his liking. 'They've got dodgers up for us in half-a-dozen states. I can't see what difference another one would make.'

'Memories are a mite short, especially lawmen's,' Belman retorted. 'If we don't give 'em cause to go digging into their stocks of dodgers they won't. Most of 'em like a quiet life anyways. If there's a posse trailing us now, I bet they haven't spread the word yet and if we salivate 'em I guess we can ride where we want without looking over our shoulders.'

Gabe Dance was still not convinced but he kept his counsel. As he stood up and crossed to the window frame that hung like a wounded arm from the wooden wall, he passed the harness that housed the golden cross and mad thoughts raced across his mind. He stood with his back to the others, staring down through the windowless gap towards the valley far below, automatically rolling a cigarette. His mind ranged over the possibilities of his riding out of Rimrock alone, with the cross his absolute property. He was so engrossed in his thoughts he did not hear Belman come up behind him but he came back to the present with a curse when Belman dashed the matches out of his hand as he was about to light his cigarette.

'You blamed fool!' Belman hissed. 'That light would show up plenty to anyone down in the valley.'

Dance turned around slowly and both men stared into each other's eyes, plumbing the depths of each other and finding treachery.

'Yeah, I guess you're right,' Dance said easily, and he moved back deeper into the dust-covered saloon. Mose Belman watched him thoughtfully and a smile played around his thin lips. It looked as though Dance would play into his hands.

Belman turned back and gazed down into the valley where the heat haze shimmered. His sharp eyes quartered every section of the view but he saw nothing. The bald eagle that plummeted down past the teetering frame shell of Rimrock to the valley had better vision, but it told Belman not to waste his time. No eagle takes its prey with men around.

The card players hardly noticed him as he crossed to the door frame from which hung one tattered remnant of the batwing doors that had seen such short service, but Dance's hot eyes followed him outside. As Belman strolled the length of Main Street, Dance moved over to the doorway and watched his leader's movements carefully. Belman gave no sign as he noticed that the old bolt-hole out of Rimrock was still holding up.

Between the splintered sides of the old assayer's office and the Blacksmith's shop he saw the opening in the rock face barely high enough for a led horse. A gap that led its tortuous way through the Little Pueblo and gave out on to a trail he had travelled before between Santa Fe and Tucson. Mose Belman knew that Dance was watching him and that the briefest show of interest in any topographical feature of Rimrock would bring his suspicious henchman on his heels, so he passed on down the street to where the dirt road slid over the rocky promontory and wound its way to the valley beneath.

Back in the saloon the card players stopped playing as though at a signal, and three of the men swivelled in their chairs to follow the gaze of Rube Holt. He was staring intently at the canvas case that held the cross and as though by common assent the four men rose up and crossed the room. Gabe Dance swung around to watch them. Holt lifted the case and carried it back to the table. Unfastening the studs that kept the canvas folds in place he slid back the flaps. The men drew in deep breaths of air as they considered the wealth that lay before them. The giant ruby winked back at them and the rings of diamonds flashed in countless colours as the daylight touched each facet. The beauty of the object was wasted upon them. All they saw was wealth unlimited.

'Get it stashed away.' Gabe Dance snarled the words, but the men made no move. Rube Holt shrugged his big shoulders and gave Dance look for look.

'I reckon it's time we cut that up six ways and shared out,' he said. 'We've got no call to stick together any longer. With that much gold we don't need any more jobs. Let's get it shared an' get to hades out of this ghost town.'

'You try telling Belman that, Rube,' Dance replied. 'He knows where we can get a price that'll double what we'd get if we carved it up.'

'Yeah, an' to get that price we've got to hole up in places like this an' mebbe take chances with a posse or two,' Holt sneered. 'If we do things Belman's way some of us will never get to taking a share. I'll settle for what I can raise from a sixth of that hunk of gold an' my share of the stones. I reckon we could draw lots for the ruby.'

'Rube's talking good sense, Gabe,' Ike Holmes, a tall, hawk-faced man said.

'Yeah, that goes for me too,' Con Marks put in.

'Me too.' Pat Lush was not given much to talking but when he said something he meant it. A shadow fell across them. Belman was back. He walked slowly to the table and glanced idly at the cross then at each man in turn.

'If you *hombres* have got any ideas of cutting that lot up you can think again. I'm not having my cut halved on account you fellers are short on patience.'

'Me neither.' Dance added his say-so vehemently and glared back when Belman's eyes mocked him. Both knew why the other wanted the cross intact.

'Can't say as I've gone against your say-so before, Mose,' Pat Lush said slowly, his face hard. 'But this time I say we share up and head in different directions.'

Belman said nothing. The ultimate decider was in his holster. No one he had met threw lead faster than Mose Belman.

'Still I guess I'll go along with you until tomorrow,' Lush continued. 'If a posse shows up by then an' we salivate 'em, so much the better but come midday tomorrow I'll be wanting what's mine.'

Holmes, Marks and Holt all nodded their agreement. Belman smiled but the humour did not reach his eyes. 'Mebbe midday to-morrow will be long enough to wait. If Lee did get help they should be pretty close by then.' He stepped between them and closing the flaps, fastened the studs and replaced the cross in its original place.

The rest of the day was spent in fitful spells of card playing and long moments of staring down into the valley for signs of pursuers. Only when night fell did Belman agree to light up the stove that still held together in the middle of the floor. By day the smoke would have given away their presence in Rimrock. By night, so long as they controlled the flames, they were safe from detection.

'I guess we'd better post a watch both ends of town,' Belman said as Lush got busy cooking a meal. 'We'll take it every two hours. Ike and Rube, you take first trick.'

The two men nodded and unpacking their slickers from their saddle-rolls, slipped out into the night.

With the meal simmering, Lush placed the iron pot he had found and scoured on the top of the stove ready for the coffee. Belman collected his mug in readiness and at the same time transferred into his cupped hand some of the Indian drug he always carried. It was a mixture of pollen and powdered bark that some Indians used in small doses to stimulate the mind whilst sleeping and to promote lurid dreams. Large doses rendered a man unconscious for anything up to forty-eight hours.

With the coffee ready Belman reached for the dip and filled his mug. In the act of setting down the mug he palmed the powder into the dip. When he returned the dip the powder fused instantly with the bubbling coffee. One after another his men filled their mugs and moved away from the stove to enjoy the bitter tang of coffee together with a smoke.

Lush was slow getting around to drinking his coffee as he fussed over the pemmican stew and beans. Belman stood up and took over the stirrer so that the man could con-centrate on his drink. He cast a covert glance at Gabe Dance and Marks and saw the fixed stare in each man's eyes and the slack jaws, the symptoms that were the forerunners of the complete blackout that followed rapidly. Calmly, Belman turned away from the stove and sat down.

Pat Lush was staggering drunkenly and Con Marks slid out of his chair to the floor. Only Gabe Dance fought against the over-powering effects of the drug. His eyes focused on Belman and the sneering smile on his leader's face expanded and diminished as the drug's phantoms were released. Vainly he strove for reason, and his hand stretched in a reflex action for a gun, then he crashed to the floor as Belman reached forward and kicked the chair from under him. Dance stayed where he was and Pat Lush stumbled and fell over the bulky form.

Mose Belman helped himself to a man-size helping of stew and hard biscuits. He ate methodically, unconcerned, stoking himself up in readiness for a long hard ride. He had no feelings when his gaze encompassed his men. They had ridden together a long time but there was no sentiment in Belman's make-up. He suffered men only so long as they were useful to him. He contemplated his next move with no twinge of conscience, and finishing his meal, strolled outside.

He walked the northern route first, stepping out firmly so that the man on watch would know he was being joined by one of the gang.

'That you, Con?' the whispered question came from Ike Holmes. He and Con Marks were pretty close.

'It's me, Belman.' The reply was easy, urbane, and Holmes stepped out of the darker shadow of the last broken-down shack that teetered on the edge of Rimrock. Belman came up close and peered along the road to where it fell away over the hill.

'Nothing stirring?' he whispered and Holmes grunted.

'Nary a thing.'

They stood together, then as Belman turned to go he froze, listening intently. Holmes caught the urgency and moved up to the edge of the road to listen. Belman's hearing was well known to the gang and Holmes reacted just as his leader anticipated. Briefly Holmes' back was outlined in front of Belman as the man strained to pick up an unusual sound. The long knife slipped into Belman's hand without a whisper of noise and the short sharp gasp that escaped Holmes' mouth as he died was lost in the rush of the everlasting wind.

Kneeling beside Holmes' body Mose Belman wiped the knife clean on the dead man's shirt, then made his way purposefully to the other end of the street. He made contact with Rube Holt and stood beside him a moment before talking. Holt was a suspicious tough customer and Belman needed to gain the man's full attention before he could engineer the situation to his requirements.

'I've been doing some thinking, Rube,' he said at length. 'It could be I'm wrong about us keeping together and getting top price for that cross. The more I think of splitting up an' going separate ways the more I like it. That way a posse will sure be set a problem.'

Rube Holt grinned in the dark. This was more like it. Belman took out a hip-flask and handed it over to the hefty Holt.

'Better take a drink of this, Rube,' he said. 'There's not enough to go round.'

Holt took the flask, and gauging the contents, drank a fairly accurate half. Reluctantly he handed the flask back.

'When do you aim to share out?' The question came eagerly.

'I guess now is as good a time as any. We can split up an' push on under cover of darkness.'

Belman turned away as if to return to the saloon and nothing loth, Holt fell in alongside him. They walked together half the distance when Belman stumbled a little, checked and continued walking. Holt was now a fraction in front, his mind centred entirely upon the fortune he would carry when he rode out. He was on his knees and crawling in the dust from the expert knife thrust before the knowledge of Belman's treachery flashed through his mind. That was the last thought Holt registered. His convulsive crawling stopped, and he stretched face down in the dust, his life blood spilling out in great spurts, until with a shudder, life itself slipped out of the big body.

This time Belman left the blood on the knife, and returning to the saloon, he placed it in Gabe Dance's hand. Dance's knife he took and placed it in his own scabbard. Unhurriedly he went to the rundown stable and saddling his mount, he led it back to the saloon and took his time packing up into his saddle-roll all the hard rations and the savings belonging to the Irish settlers. After fastening the roll behind his saddle cantle, he returned for the cross. He was thankful for the thoroughness of the Irish saddler who had fitted shoulder straps to the casing, and as he struggled into the harness his eyes glistened at the weight of it.

Picking up one of the spare blankets he draped it from the saddle so that it would obliterate his trail, then without a backward glance Mose Belman led his horse out of Rimrock, through the long torturous fissure towards the old Spanish trail.

It needed just three hours to sundown the next day when Sheriff Luke Vane drew rein in Rimrock valley and pointed significantly to where two groups of buzzards hopped and flapped over a feast up on the escarpment. His deputies grouped around him, but they read the signs for themselves.

'I guess we'll take a look-see,' Vane said briefly. 'Could be we'll pick up a trail from there.'

Jack Grout laughed nastily. 'If there's a trail from there it'll show in the valley one side or another. That road just goes straight up, through and down again.'

Vane ignored the man's remark. He was bitterly regretting having sworn in this hard-bitten crew, and was now under no delusions concerning their intentions, but he was a dogged, persistent lawman, and nothing deflected him from trying to do his job. The sheriff edged his mount in front again and headed towards the steady gradient leading up to the ghost town of Rimrock. When they were halfway up the slope the buzzards rose like a couple of black clouds and commenced their spiralling climb that would take them almost out of sight.

It was then that Gabe Dance aroused himself out of his drugged stupor and stared around the saloon. He struggled into a sitting position causing Pat Lush to roll to the floor and the stained knife dropped out of Dance's hand. His gaze fastened on the knife as his mind struggled to bridge the gap in time, and memory flooded back. The significance of the stained knife registered and he turned to examine Lush and Con Marks. They stirred as he turned them over and getting to his feet, he prodded them until their eyelids flickered.

Gabe Dance felt white-hot rage well up in him as he realized how easily Belman had duped him. The fact that he was still in one piece failed to cause him satisfaction, yet had he been able to implement his own plan, no one would have been spared. Savagely he glared across the saloon to where the cross had lain and his loss in terms of wealth caused him almost physical pain. He was about to yell at Lush and Marks when he heard the approaching horsemen. His mind whirled as he realized Belman had been right and the posse was right here, and he, Gabe Dance, had been left as a sacrifice.

He reacted just the way Mose Belman would have liked. Without hesitation he dragged at his guns and staggered to the doorway. The half-dozen horsemen grouped behind the lawman who stood examining the remnants of clothing and almost clean skeleton that a day earlier had been Rube Holt, neither saw nor heard Dance appear. His guns thundered and Luke Vance's tenure as Sheriff of Amarillo ended as he joined what remained of Rube Holt.

Two other men pitched out of their saddles

as the riders got caught up in a mêlée in their eagerness to find cover. The four remaining riders disentangled themselves and crouching low, rode behind the nearest building. Jack Grout was firing as he brought up the rear and his second bullet smashed into Gabe Dance's shoulder. A spasm of pain crossed Dance's face but he held on. When the guns started in earnest from across the street, he staggered back inside the building for cover.

Lush and Marks were on their feet and staring wild-eyed at Dance. His pain-wracked eyes appealed to them for help and he jerked his head savagely towards the other side of the street. 'The posse,' he snarled. 'Belman drugged us and got clear with the cross.'

Lush and Marks were still too bemused to have any opinions about Belman, but the bullets thudding into the woodwork roused their natural fighting instincts, and palming their guns they searched for suitable cover. They pulled the table up to the window, and upending it, ducked behind, and stayed, waiting for a target to show.

Jack Grout and his three henchmen made the cardinal mistake of underestimating the strength of the enemy. Having seen only one man they concluded he was the sole obstacle between them and the prize they coveted, the cross. Waving his men back out of the rear of the building, Grout instructed them to spread and close in upon the saloon from both sides.

There was a lull when Gabe Dance pushed another table up to the doorway, then Grout came in a swerving run, his guns blazing. Dance was too slow taking cover and when he dropped behind the table, he had a neat round hole in his forehead. Lush fired once and Grout spun a couple of times before ploughing into the dust. His men poured a fusillade of lead into the woodwork and Con Marks coughed blood as he slid to the floor.

The blood lust spilled up in Pat Lush and swinging the table aside he jumped clear through the window frame. Crouching low he swung his guns in an arc. The lone man on the left-hand died with two slugs in his heart and Lush turned like a cat to face the other two. Dust spurted up around him as bullets ploughed into the ground but Lush was oblivious to danger. His big Colts jerked as he took aim at the two remaining men. The opposition melted away like snowflakes in a hot sun but Pat Lush's luck dried up right there. The mists cleared briefly from Jack Grout's eyes and raising his head he saw Pat Lush crouched in front of him.

With an effort he raised a gun and tried to steady his aim. The mists closed down again and his target faded from view but doggedly Grout pressed the trigger. Lush's sixth sense warned him of danger and he whirled around to face the threat. The bullet ploughed its way into his body and he slipped on to his knees, clutching his stomach with hands that turned red instantly, then with a moan he keeled over to lie face upwards, staring with sightless eyes.

CHAPTER FOUR

Mex Juarez reined his pinto to a stop, and Bellamy, a questioning look on his face, did likewise. The Mexican's head was tilted slightly as he listened. Clint grinned and left him to it. They had been long enough together for the Texan to trust his pardner's acute hearing and assessment of what the sounds portended.

'Sounds like we're being followed, an' I'd guess by a coupla settlers ridin' those big cayuses.'

Clint Bellamy made no reply but sat his mount with shoulders hunched, peering back trail for sight of the men who followed them. The sun had gone down and the shadows shrouded the trail that hugged close to the steep hill, so that the sound of approaching riders was clearly audible to the Texan before they came into view. The pardners exchanged glances when the two Irishmen rode out of the murk. There was a purposeful air about the newcomers and they had the look of men who would not easily be diverted from their course.

'You fellers sure moved some,' the big, ginger-headed Irishman remarked when

51

they pulled their cumbersome mounts to a stop. 'We looked like spending the night on our own.'

'Well you've caught up. Now what do you want?' Clint put the question with a marked lack of interest.

'We aim to help you get that cross back.' It was the other, black-visaged Irishman who answered, and his brow beetled with anger when both Clint and Mex laughed.

'What's your interest in the cross?' Mex asked. 'Are you so eager to see it fixed up in some church that you'll risk your lives chasing it? Or do you aim on getting rich quick?'

'We could ask you that,' the ginger-haired man growled. 'We came along so that we can keep an eye on it.'

Mex held up his hand for silence and after listening briefly turned back to the settlers. There was an amused glint in his eyes. 'A couple more *hombres* coming forking the same breed of cayuse. Seems they don't trust you two to return the cross if you ever get it.'

The Irishmen looked nonplussed. They could hear nothing, but they had no cause to doubt him. Clint heaved a deep sigh of exasperation. There would be difficulties enough ahead of them without nursing four greenhorns. The feeling bordered on anger when the two newcomers emerged out of the gloom. Young Matt Sullivan could be a help at a pinch but the girl riding alongside him could be nothing but a problem.

'And where in blazes are you going?' Clint asked harshly when the boy and girl reined in. Matt Sullivan had the grace to look a little shame-faced as he nodded towards the other two men.

'I heard Jamie Reardon and Mike Kelly say they were coming to help you and I thought perhaps you could use some more help.'

Clint nodded, his eyes like ice-chips. 'And so you bring a young girl away from the safety of the wagon train on the trail of thieves and killers. You'll have a full-time chore looking after her so it's precious little help you'll be to us.'

Matt Sullivan said nothing but the girl stared at Clint with a savagery that shocked the Texan.

'Nobody brings Kathy Mullins anywhere, Mister Bellamy,' she ground out in a husky, throaty voice. 'I came became I'm not letting Matt Sullivan out of my sight ever again.'

Clint exhaled a hissing breath and searched his pockets for his tobacco pouch. Lighting the hastily rolled cigarette he saw what had not escaped the eagle eyes of Mex Juarez. Reardon and Kelly were looking at the girl with undisguised lust. The Texan groaned inwardly. What had been a straight-forward manhunt was now fast developing complications.

'Tag along if you want,' Mex said finally. 'But if we don't catch up with Dance an' his men by sundown tomorrow we'll head back for the wagon train.' He turned his pinto around as he spoke and gigged it into action. Clint followed without another look at the settlers and the lumbering Irish horses clattered noisily behind.

The last of the daylight faded as Mex led the way on to a narrow deer trail that led up the face of the mountain and through to the inner ring of the Little Pueblos where the pards expected to pick up the trail of Gabe Dance and his men, and they were eager to reach a good starting point before camping for the night. Behind them, the big horses slithered and stumbled when the trail narrowed, and Reardon and Kelly mouthed curses, but neither the Mexican nor the Texan paid any attention to them.

When they rounded the breast of the hill the moon slid into view, showing the trail ahead as it wound its way down the inner slopes of the mountain. This was fortuitous, because the Irish horses were finding downhill harder than uphill. Both Clint and Mex were relieved when they hit the bottom of the grade and turned north-west to follow the foot of the hills. They kept on, ignoring the talk of food and rest behind them, until they arrived at a point where water trickled out of a craggy section of outcrop.

Reardon and Kelly climbed down from their saddles and straight away set about making inroads into provisions they had carried. Matt Sullivan and Kathy Mullins followed the example of the Westerners and attended first to their horses' needs. The girl wore an enveloping woollen garment with a riding hood and her big eyes stared up at the pards uncertainly. Matt Sullivan, still shame-faced, found difficulty in looking at them squarely. After watering their mounts they led them to where the bunch-grass grew in sufficient quantity and the other two Irish horses moved eagerly to where the water ran on the surface before the greedy earth sucked it under and Mex turned his attention on Reardon and Kelly.

'You *hombres* can get off your fans an' see to those cayuses,' he remarked quietly. 'If they take in too much water they're gonna get colic, an' a man doesn't stand much chance in this territory without a cayuse.'

Reardon snarled angrily and hauled himself to his feet. He stalked up to where the two animals had their muzzles in the ice-cold liquid and planted a heavy boot into the under-belly of the nearest one, sending it scrambling backwards. His foot was coming back again when the Mexican grasped it in a steer-throwing grip and sent him heavily to the ground. Reardon came up slowly, his fighting instinct aroused. He crossed the distance between him and Mex in a second then stopped, his eyes fastened on the six inches of cold steel in the Mexican's hand.

'Any *hombre* who treats a cayuse that way is plain scum, mister!' Mex hissed. 'You do that agin an' I'll carve "scum" on that fat belly you tote around.'

Kelly made to get behind the Mexican but froze when Clint's gun dug deep into his back.

'You can talk big when you're holding the knife,' Reardon growled, his face contorted with rage. 'I'd beat you to a pulp just man to man.'

Mex shrugged. 'That's as maybe, just remember I've got the knife. Now get the saddles off those cayuses an' get them staked out where there's enough grass.'

Reardon stared obstinately until Mex made a move forward with the knife extended, then the Irishman moved away to do as he was told.

Sheathing his knife Mex turned away and started collecting deadwood for a fire. Clint holstered his gun and Kelly subsided back to his place beside a small boulder. An uneasy silence settled around them as Mex started the fire going and rigged up the coffee pot. Reardon and Kelly sat together, staring belligerently at the pards whilst Matt Sullivan and Kathy Mullins sat on the perimeter of light cast by the fire, awkward and ill at ease.

Somewhere up in the Little Pueblos a cougar roared and Kathy Mullins shivered as she moved nearer the fire. Its mate answered and the girl moved again until she sat close up to Reardon. Matt moved alongside her, staring moodily into the firelight. He looked as though he was regretting having followed Reardon and Kelly.

When the coffee was ready Mex filled up their mugs. The girl looked so forlorn that his handsome face split into a smile as he handed her a mug, and moisture sprang to her eyes as her defence mechanism slipped a little. Mex resumed his seat and watched the settlers out of half-closed eyes. Reardon had given up staring at the pards. His attention was now given over to Kathy Mullins. The girl's nearness was having its effect upon him and he was almost slavering as the flames highlighted her features. Unwittingly she pushed her hood back and her thick, black, wavy hair glistened in the light. Involuntarily, Reardon inched nearer to her.

Mex opened one eye fully and looked up at his pard who was busy rolling himself a cigarette. Clint's eye flickered and the Mexican was content. He knew that Bellamy would keep careful watch for the next couple of hours, so he pulled a blanket over himself and went to sleep. The Texan passed his tobacco sack to Matt Sullivan when the youngster sniffed at the smoke hungrily, and when Sullivan had built a clumsy-looking cigarette, Clint held up a piece of burning timber. Matt Sullivan's smile of appreciation was warm and the Texan grinned back.

With their cigarettes smoked both men tossed the butts into the flames, and whilst Clint merely rested against a boulder, the others settled down to sleep. Matt Sullivan, out of propriety, moved further away from Kathy Mullins but Reardon squirmed around until he was within an arm's length of her.

The red-haired Irishman's gaze was directed towards the girl with the intensity of a snake and when she fell into a deep sleep, the sweat stood out of his face as he watched the gentle rise and fall of her breasts. A couple of hours passed by and Clint placed more deadwood on the fire. He nudged his pard once and immediately the Mexican's eyes opened. He nodded imperceptibly and Clint left him to the chore of watching Reardon.

It was the Irishman's scream of pain that dragged the Texan and the others from sleep. Juarez was standing over Reardon who had the Mexican's knife clean through the hand that had reached out to the unsuspecting girl. The Irishman was staring in disbelief at the blade that dripped red blood protruding from his palm, and mouthing curses incoherently. Kathy Mullins sat upright and stared uncomprehending until understanding dawned. She picked up her blankets and without hesitation sat between Sullivan and Clint Bellamy.

Mex held his Colt to the Irishman's temple as he leaned over to grasp the handle of his knife and Reardon blanched as he struggled to control his rage. Savagely the Mexican pulled his knife free and Reardon gave a yell of pain, then clasped his hand to his chest.

'Next time, feller, an' I'll leave you staked for buzzard meat.' The Mexican turned away as he spoke and after rummaging in his saddlebag he tossed a wide bandage across to Kelly. 'Better get that hole covered up for your sidekick before he bleeds to death.'

For ten minutes or more Kelly struggled at bandaging Reardon's hand while Reardon called him all sorts of a clumsy fool, then the uneasy silence settled down again but this time Reardon had more to think about than Kathy Mullins' charms. His occasional groan went unremarked.

Clint and Mex were up well before dawn and when the others finally awoke, the morning air carried the sharp tang of coffee. Kathy Mullins sat up and shivered as she looked around, her big, blue eyes wide as she took stock of her surroundings. Clint handed her a mug of scalding coffee. 'Get outside that, Miss,' he said with a grin. 'Then maybe things'll look a little better.'

She smiled and clasped the mug so that it warmed her hands. Matt Sullivan stirred, rubbing his eyes, but Reardon and Kelly still slept. Clint watched the girl as she sipped the hot liquid carefully, and Mex, who was watering the horses, eyed his pardner's concern with amusement.

'Didn't your folks try to stop you riding away from the wagon train?' Clint asked. He rolled himself a cigarette as though the question was secondary to his interest in the tobacco. The girl made no reply for some time and Clint cursed himself for a clumsy fool when he saw that she was struggling with her emotions.

'I've no folk left, Mr Bellamy,' she said at length. 'My mother died five years ago, and my father was shot by the men who stole the cross.'

Clint nodded slowly and as he filled a mug for Matt Sullivan he remembered the youngster having said that two of the settlers had been killed trying to stop Gabe Dance and his men. He reckoned that Kathy Mullins had as much gall as her father, and he warmed to the girl.

Reardon and Kelly woke up and after sending surly glances at the pards, ate their hard tack in silence. As soon as they were finished Clint and Mex herded them around the bulge of the hill along with Matt

Sullivan, whilst the girl remained at the water to freshen herself in privacy.

About an hour after sunup they were in the saddle all ready to move off. Clint turned and caught the attention of the settlers. His expression was grim, and for once he allowed the full measure of authority to creep into his manner. 'From now we'll be taking the chance of running into the men we're trailing. They don't rate life too high an' they'd salivate us like it was a chore of work, so we'll only keep healthy by travelling without noise an' that means no talking.'

Nobody spoke and by the expressions on the faces of the settlers it seemed they took his words seriously, so he turned his big gelding around and followed his pardner.

At midday they sheltered from the sun under the concave walls of a little canyon and ate sparingly from their ration supply. Under Clint's watchful eye they washed the meal down with a few mouthfuls of water. Just outside the entrance to the canyon, Mex squatted on his hunkers, keeping his eye on the horses cropping without enthusiasm at the sparse dried bunch-grass. Smoking one of his cheroots he contemplated the Irish horses with concern. His experienced eye told him that for all their size they would need careful nurturing; they contrasted badly with the pinto and dun gelding, the true prairie stock.

Judging the animals had foraged sufficiently, he led them back into the canyon and silently the uneasy group of settlers climbed into their saddles. Mex rode away out in front whilst Clint took up the rear position. Young Matt Sullivan and Kathy Mullins were oblivious to the discomforts in the pleasure they found in each other's company. They found no need to talk, their understanding having reached the point when the eyes had a language all of their own. Watching them, the Texan hoped that things would work out well for them in their adopted country.

Every now and again, Reardon turned in the saddle to stare at the girl, his face contorted with jealousy as Kathy ignored him. His whole expression boded ill for Matt Sullivan and Clint decided to watch the situation closely, then when Mex halted, he rode past the Irishman to join his pard.

'We're on the right trail, Clint.' Mex nodded towards the rocky trail that came down from the hill that separated them from the dusty bowl of the Amarillo Desert. At the intersection of the trails there were marks of fairly recent origin, where shod horses had slithered the last few feet to level ground. Mex dismounted and studied the trail intently. When he climbed back into the saddle there was a smile on his handsome face.

'The way I see it, Dance and his men passed this way a couple of days ahead of

Vane's posse, and Vane's no more than an hour ahead of us, so we did right taking the outside route.'

'We're not going to do any good getting close to Vane with these greenhorns,' Clint remarked at length. 'We'd better split up an' get the settlers back to the wagon train.'

Mex shook his head. 'It might come to that but I've been thinking what I'd do in Dance's place,' he replied. 'He knows that Jim Lee got away when they killed Dorgan, Ringo and Borg, an' mebbe he's expecting Lee to bring the law on his trail. I guess I'd hole up somewhere and fix any lawman that showed up. That way I'd gain time to clear out of the territory and trade in that hunk of gold.'

'That makes sense, but who knows where he'd make a stand?' Clint queried.

'Somewhere this side of Santa Fe I guess. With Vane just ahead of us, we could be on hand when the trouble pops.'

'There's a lot of territory between here and Santa Fe,' remarked Clint. He was about to press the intention to split up when his memory brought him in tune with his pardner. 'I've got a hunch you're expecting to find Dance holed up at that ghost town we caught sight of on our way down, place called Rimrock.'

'You're durned right,' Mex agreed. 'If Dance knows the territory, then Rimrock's the place he'd choose.'

The Texan rolled himself a smoke as he considered things, then edged his mount upwind of Juarez as the Mexican lit up one of his cheroots. 'That shanty town of Rimrock is no more than a couple of hours ride from here, Mex. When we round the shoulder of the hill we should get a sight of it, and anyone up in Rimrock will have a pretty clear view of us if we keep to the low ground.'

Mex shrugged his shoulders. 'Can't see that it matters. Vane and his posse won't get sight of us, and the *hombres* up in Rimrock will only have eyes for the lawmen. We should see what happens without pushing our luck.'

Clint nodded agreement, and while Mex moved off towards the distant shoulder of the hill he waited for the settlers.

Clint's memory had not deceived him. When they rounded the shoulder of the hill Rimrock showed briefly through the haze. The rolling terrain that ran to the foot of the unscaleable mountain behind Rimrock hid Sheriff Vane and his posse from sight. After half an hour's riding Rimrock emerged completely out of the shimmering haze, a Rimrock as peaceful-looking as a tomb.

They caught the first sight of Vane and his men when the sheriff was no more than two miles from the foot of the trail that climbed up to the little township. The posse was moving carefully, taking cover from every patch of brush and fold of terrain as they closed the distance.

Vane and his men stopped some short distance away from the road to Rimrock and for long minutes they were bunched, surveying the hill and gimcrack buildings intently. When they started the ride up the slope both Clint and Mex had seen what had encouraged them to move into the open so boldly. Above the frame buildings of Rimrock heavy-bodied buzzards rose up and fluttered back down as they squabbled over a feast. Things seemed to have happened in Rimrock.

The riders breasted the hill unhurriedly and the buzzards rose up in a cloud at their approach. The frame buildings hid Vane and his men from view for a time when nothing happened, then the sounds of gunfire drifted back to the watching men. For five minutes the shooting went on, then it stopped as suddenly as it had started.

'Some battle,' murmured Clint, his eyes glued on the in-and-out trail of Rimrock. Mex merely grunted. Like Clint, he was expecting someone to ride out toting the cross. There just had to be some outcome from all that gunplay.

Matt Sullivan and the girl had moved up close beside Clint and Mex as though to draw confidence from the men who were used to gunplay, but Jamie Reardon and Mike Kelly had drawn away. They too hoped that the shooting meant the cross was not far away. The glances both men kept shooting towards the others boded ill for the men, and not much better for Kathy Mullins.

Minutes dragged by, but nothing moved in Rimrock. Mex glanced up to the sky and Clint followed his gaze. The buzzards were in sight again, mere dots circling, ever circling and coming down.

CHAPTER FIVE

When the buzzards reached rooftop level the pards decided it was time to move in. 'You folk had better wait here until we give you the all-clear,' Clint suggested as he re-mounted his big gelding.

Jamie Reardon, the massive, ginger-headed Irishman, pushed forward. 'Yeah! And let you get away with the cross!' he snarled. 'Not likely!'

Clint shrugged his shoulders. 'Suit yourself,' he said briefly, his gaze resting frostily on Reardon. A glance passed between the two pards and they led the way out from the cover of the mesquite clump. When they started up the slope to Rimrock, Mex took the lead, but Clint dropped behind to keep an eye on the two Irishmen. He knew that given the opportunity either man would kill for the sake of the Spanish cross.

The buzzards soared angrily as Mex topped the hill and held his pinto motion-less while he surveyed the length of Rim-rock. It took a lot to shake the Mexican's equanimity, but the carnage in Rimrock appalled him. He would have preferred that Kathy Mullins was spared the sight, but it was better that they all stayed together. He turned in the saddle and motioned the others forward. Reardon and Kelly pulled alongside him and stared down the street, their faces suddenly pale and drawn. Matt Sullivan blanched and held out his hand to Kathy Mullins in a comforting gesture. The girl shuddered in undisguised horror.

Clint and Mex dismounted and taking a side each, made their careful way down the street. By the time they had gone a third of the way along the two Irishmen could not stand the strain of waiting and dropping to the ground heavily, followed in the wake of the Westerners. When they passed the dead men littered along the dusty road they averted their eyes from the harvest of greed.

Ten minutes later the pards were satisfied that no gunman lurked in the shadows. At each end of town lay a skeleton, almost cleanly picked. Seven more men lay dead in the street and in what had once been a saloon, two men were slumped amidst the overturned chairs and tables. It was such a scene of slaughter that even the hardened Westerners were shocked. Reardon and Kelly were now so intent upon getting their hands on the prize that they ignored the corpses littering the scene. While Clint and Mex surveyed the saloon carefully, the Irishmen charged around from point to point expecting at any moment to uncover the cross.

Their disappointment grew with every minute's futile search, then, disbelief showing in every line of their features, they left the saloon to start a systematic search of every building.

The pardners returned to the street and checked on the dead men. Sheriff Vane and his bunch of deputies they recognized; the others were strangers. Clint motioned Matt Sullivan to join them and the lad dismounted, closing the distance almost on tiptoe in respect for the dead.

'You seen these before, Matt?' Clint asked, indicating one body in the street and pointing towards the saloon.

Matt Sullivan looked closely at the body and nodded. 'Yes, he's one of the killers who robbed the wagon train. They called him Pat Lush.' The lad went into the saloon and returned soon after. 'Those two as well,' he continued. 'One's Gabe Dance and the other's Con Marks.'

'Allowing for the buzzard meat at each end of town that accounts for all of 'em,' Mex said quietly.

'Vane and his posse an' all of the *hombres* who shot up Borg, Dorgan and the others.'

Clint Bellamy pushed his sombrero back and scratched his head in perplexity. There were two horses standing desultorily in the street, four others were behind the flimsy buildings and five more were in the rough

69

stable they had checked on their first scrutiny of Rimrock.

'Yeah, it sure does,' he replied. 'And there's a bronc apiece for them so that ties it up. One thing's sure, nobody came out of this burg after the fracas.'

'We'd better give things a closer look.' Mex glanced to where the girl still sat astride her big, drooping draught-horse as he spoke. He turned to Matt Sullivan. 'Get the girl into one of the buildings while we take another look around and clean up this place a mite.'

Matt nodded and went back to the girl with considerable eagerness. Reardon and Kelly clattered in and out of buildings muttering and mouthing their disappointment, then as Clint and Mex showed signs of searching the place again the Irishman hurried to join them and returned the glances from the pards with stares of open hostility.

Neither Westerner spoke as they moved slowly through Rimrock. Just a glance now and again from one to the other conveyed the significance of some sign that had escaped them earlier. Reardon and Kelly were breathing down their necks at every turn, but neither knew at the end of the search what Mex and Clint had divined.

At the gimcrack stable where five horses nosed into almost empty mangers, Mex's eagle eyes had seen where a sixth harness had hung recently. Knowing now what to look for

70

the pards gave closer attention to the old dirt trail beyond the stable. The lone rider had covered his tracks well but had missed two light scores in the hard rock where he had led his horse off the road towards the low narrow break in the cliffs just beyond what had been the assayer's office and the blacksmith's shop. The Mexican's keen eyes took in the marks and the break in the cliffs in a swift all-embracing glance, and continued searching along the main road of Rimrock with such care that the Irishmen had no clue of the discovery. Reaching the steep incline down to the valley, Mex stopped and shrugged his shoulders resignedly.

'We might as well get back to the wagon train,' he said. 'We've come to the end of the trail. Every last one of the *hombres* we've trailed is dead.'

'Not so fast mister. We're not leaving without that cross.' Kelly towered menacingly over Mex as he blurted out the words, but the Mexican smiled easily.

'I'm thinking you're going to be plumb unlucky. I'll bet my last cent you won't find the cross in this place an' somehow I think you'd be more unlucky if you did.'

'Why more unlucky?' Kelly asked, his black eyebrows furrowing.

'Just look around,' Mex replied. 'All those *hombres* died on account of that cross. All maybe except Sheriff Vane. He was just doing a chore of work.'

Both Reardon and Kelly eyed the corpses without enthusiasm.

'Seems bad luck's followed that cross ever since it was taken from wherever it was first used. I'd sure hate to tote it around.' Clint's voice carried a tone of honest conviction but the Irishmen snorted their disbelief.

'You'd tote it, mister, if you could lay your thieving hands on it,' Reardon gritted savagely. 'Don't think you're going to fox us into giving up the search.'

'Search all you want,' the Texan replied. 'But later. You'll take your shares in the chores first, an' that means getting those *hombres* buried.'

'They can wait!' Reardon snarled. 'They're in no hurry.' He turned to go, then froze as Clint's gun appeared with smooth speed.

'The only reason they'll wait is on account we'll be putting you away first. Make your choice.'

'Those guns don't leave any choice but I'll tear you apart with these, mister, before we're through.' The Irishman spread his huge hands, the one still heavily bandaged, but Clint looked unimpressed.

'Maybe I'll give you the pleasure of trying sometime,' he said quietly, then, 'Well come on! Let's get the job done.'

With bad grace the two Irishmen lent a hand in gathering the corpses together. Mex searched the clothing and made a bundle out of letters and money, whilst Clint made a note of the value of each man's possessions. Sheriff Vane's clothing and money-belt yielded vastly less than any of the others, a sad reflection upon the benefits of virtue and law abiding. Mex added the sheriff's badge to the pile then tied up the bundle with a length of leather thong.

'And what are you aiming to do with that lot?' Kelly's pig-eyes bored into Mex as he spoke. The Mexican's reply was terse.

'We're gonna hand them over to the law at the first township we hit. Somewhere maybe, someone wants to know what happened to these *hombres.*'

'Sure!' Kelly's face was distorted in a sneer. 'It's right enough to hand in the details, but the money, we might as well split it.'

Mex did not bother to answer but reaching his pinto, rolled the bundle in his saddle-roll. The Irishmen watched him out of hot, greedy eyes.

They buried the dead men in a communal grave under a cairn of stones, with the exception of Sheriff Vane's body. This they buried alone as Clint and Mex reckoned he deserved to keep better company in death.

Just a little lower down the Rimrock trail beyond the stable, water bubbled out of the rocks and with the fodder Matt Sullivan collected before nightfall from the valley, they were able to supply the needs of the horses. By the time night closed in they were all gathered in the saloon that had housed Belman and his men. The doped coffee-pot they threw out together with all other evidence of the gang's stay and used their own implements to rustle up a meal.

After supper Clint rigged up a blanket screen across a corner of the room for the girl to settle down. Reardon and Kelly drew themselves close to the stove fire then glared in almost apoplectic rage as the Texan gave them their marching orders.

'You two *hombres* can settle yourselves anywhere you like except in this place,' he said peremptorily. 'Get going!'

Reardon went to dive for Clint then stopped with a snort of disgust as the Texan's guns slid into his hands. His eyes were bitter. 'I reckon you're bluffing, mister,' he said slowly. 'You go ahead and shoot. I'm not stirring from here.'

Clint's smile widened as the Irishman stared back. He made no apparent attempt to take aim but the bullet he fired seared the first layer of skin to make an inch long weal in Reardon's neck. Reardon squealed like a stuck pig and clapping his hand to his injured neck, jumped to his feet and grabbed his bedding with his good hand. Mike Kelly was a split second behind him as he blundered out into the night.

'You are making bad enemies, Mister Bellamy.' Matt Sullivan's long face was solemn as he spoke. 'Never let Reardon or Kelly catch you without your guns handy. They're powerful men.'

Mex laughed heartily. 'Don't lose sleep none on account of Clint. I'll lay you an even dollar that Reardon an' Kelly would lose even without the fire-irons.'

Matt Sullivan's eyes held a lot of doubt for some time, but eventually the calm easy-going manner of the two pards convinced him and he settled down for the night. Soon he was sound asleep, and from behind the screen the pards could hear Kathy Mullins' rhythmic breathing. She too was fast asleep.

'What do you make of the *hombre* who got out through the back door?' Clint asked quietly.

Mex drew hard on his cheroot before answering. 'Well, there's only one feller who hasn't been accounted for yet.' Clint squinted at his suave companion as he rolled himself a smoke. It looked like Mex had formed the same opinion as himself.

'...and that's the priest who called himself Father Dewar,' Mex continued. 'What was it Sheriff Vane said about Dance? He shot up an escort taking in Mose Belman to Fort Munro. Could be this Belman and Father Dewar are one and the same, the bossman of the outfit.'

'Yeah, and judging from what happened to the two fellers each end of Rimrock he'll kill at the drop of a hat.'

'Judging from where they died,' said Mex, 'I'd say they were on look-out, an' died at the hands of someone they trusted.'

The pards relapsed into silence for a while, both busy with the same problem. Clint was halfway through his second cigarette before making up his mind. He was prepared to give way however if Mex should opt for the only other acceptable alternative.

'I'm thinking we'll have to push on after the *hombre* who got away and tote these folk along with us. It'd take a few days before we could join up again if one of us headed back to the wagon train.'

'You're plumb right,' Mex agreed. 'My guess is that Belman or Dewar is gonna take some finding even if we get after him at sunup.'

With the decision made they settled down. If the responsibility of wet-nursing the immigrants on the trail of a cold-blooded killer weighed down on them at all, it did not register.

Long before sunup Clint and Mex were up and busy. The two youngsters stirred only when the smell of coffee filled the air. Matt Sullivan unwound his long legs and surveyed the pardners with an apologetic air.

'You should have given me a shake and I

could have helped,' he said.

Mex passed a mug of coffee to the youngster and grinned away the lad's discomfiture.

'When we need you to lend a hand we'll sure enough let you know,' he said easily, then as Kathy Mullins pulled aside the blanket, 'Come right out, ma'am. I guess you could sure use some chow.'

The night's sleep had done the girl a lot of good. Her eyes held a special brightness as she took the mug of coffee Mex proffered and moved towards the chair Matt Sullivan placed beside him. When they were halfway through their breakfast, Reardon and Kelly lumbered in, and almost drooled at the sight of the flapjacks that sizzled gently in the pan. They stopped a couple of yards away from the others, uncertain how to get back on a good enough footing to get amongst the food, they were both taken aback when Clint nodded to the pan.

'Help yourselves,' he said with no trace of rancour in his voice.

The two men shrugged away their surprise and sharing the rest of the flapjacks between them, took up positions some distance away from the others. They ate in silence and later filled their mugs with coffee without any attempt at conversation, but all the time they watched Clint and Mex with hot, hate-filled eyes.

With breakfast finished, Reardon and Kelly

stood up and started for the door, eager to recommence their search. They turned with snarls of impatience when Mex called out to them.

'You *hombres* can stay here until Miss Kathy gets herself freshened up,' he instructed. His eyes ran lazily over both men, daring them to disobey, and for a full minute it looked as though they would, then with bad grace they sat back down. The Mexican turned to Kathy Mullins.

'You'll find water a short way down the road, coming out of the rock face. Fix yourself up in any of the buildings and we'll stay right here until you're through.'

The girl flashed him a grateful look as she hurried outside. Reardon's hot glance followed her, his desire stronger than the throbbing pain still pulsating in the hand Mex had stabbed. When she disappeared he turned his gaze slowly to meet the Mexican's stare for stare.

'When Miss Kathy's through you can take the cayuses down to the valley and let 'em find what graze they can.' Clint tossed his tobacco sac to Matt as he spoke and the youngster nodded eagerly.

'Sure thing, Mister Bellamy,' he replied as he fumbled with tobacco and paper. Lighting the badly constructed cigarette he grinned ruefully when Clint eyed it humorously. 'Looks like I'm a greenhorn at most things,' he added.

'You'll learn. All it takes is time,' Clint remarked. 'But rolling smokes is way down on the list of things you'll need to learn in this territory.'

They smoked in silence for some time, Sullivan and the pards relaxed and contented but Reardon and Kelly edgy and impatient. Clint finally broke the silence.

'As soon as the cayuses are ready we'll move out.'

'Yeah, and when you get us out of the way, you'll come back for the cross,' Kelly blurted out. 'No, mister! We'll stay right here until we find it.'

'Sure! You stay! We didn't ask you to horn in on us in the first place.' Mex's tone was silky. 'If you're calling the tune you can become buzzard meat for all we care.'

Kathy Mullins came back into the one-time saloon and Kelly and Reardon rushed outside to carry on with their search. The pards watched them go, the glint of amusement in their eyes. Matt Sullivan went out immediately to attend to the horses, leaving Clint and Mex to clean up and get ready for the trail. Kathy Mullins watched them as they worked unhurriedly. They looked utterly dependable and the girl warmed to them.

'I'm sorry we followed you and added to your problems,' she said after a while, and was immediately gratified by their warm smiles.

Clint rubbed his chin reflectively. 'Well now, any problems you might have brought are more than compensated by your company, ma'am. We're mighty pleased to have you along.'

A warm flush of pleasure rose up from the girl's neck. 'You might as well know why we came,' she went on. 'Matt heard Reardon and Kelly plotting to take the cross for themselves, and after what you did for him, he wanted to warn you, and like I said, I'm sticking close to Matt for keeps.'

'We're obliged to you for telling us,' Mex said kindly. 'I sure hated to think he was fool enough to lead you away from the wagon train without a mighty good reason.'

'Matt is no fool,' she replied quickly. 'I wouldn't waste any time on him if he were.'

The pards grinned at her vehemence, and having finished the chores, sat down to enjoy a smoke. The easy charm of the Westerners got the girl talking freely, releasing the pent-up well of emotion that her father's death had created, and they listened, completely entranced. She enlarged upon the grim conditions that had forced the entire population of Droghadee to leave Ireland and the hopes of founding a new thriving community somewhere in the Americas, and so absorbed were the pards, that Matt Sullivan was back from the valley with the horses before they moved.

Kelly and Reardon emerged from a shack that sagged on rotting floorboards as the others prepared to move out, and stared sullenly as the horses were saddled up. Mex sorted out a couple of the best animals that had carried Dance and his men and Luke Vane and his posse for Matt and Kathy. The other animals they tethered one to another, attaching the leader to Clint's gelding.

'You *hombres* had better get moving,' Mex growled as he swung into the saddle.

'We'll come when we've found what we're looking for,' Reardon replied.

Mex shrugged his shoulders. 'Suit yourselves. You'll find two good cayuses and your broncs in the stable.'

The Irishmen did not answer and doubt flitted across their heavy features. Clint leaned over in the saddle to catch their eyes. 'You spend too much time looking for that hunk of gold an' you'll die on account of it. My advice is to ride back to the wagon train while the route is fresh in your minds.'

Neither Matt Sullivan nor Kathy Mullins said anything to their countrymen as Mex rode down the rough road in the lead of the long cavalcade of ridden and riderless horses. The motives of Kelly and Reardon placed them beyond the pale and the youngsters looked woodenly ahead as they moved away.

When Mex dismounted between the old assay office and blacksmith's shop, both Kelly and Reardon stepped well out into the road to watch. Reardon's rifle was in his hands and his expression showed he would shoot to kill if the Westerners unearthed the cross at that point. The expressions of hate and mistrust turned to incredulity as Mex then led the way into the cliff face. The two men followed down the roadway and stared as the last horse passed from sight.

'I thought those fellers were heading back for the wagon train,' Kelly gritted. 'Where in blazes are they going?'

'They're bluffing,' Reardon shouted. 'They're banking on us heading back to the wagon train then they'll come right back and pick up the cross.'

'That sounds like sense, Jamie,' Kelly rejoined. 'C'mon, the sooner we find it the better.'

They spent an aimless hour poking around the buildings with the uncomfortable feeling of loneliness rising inside them. The ghostly aura of Rimrock increased rather than diminished under the torrid sun and at last they could stand it no longer. Kelly suggested they should perhaps follow the others through the mountain, and Reardon was only too glad to agree.

CHAPTER SIX

Mose Belman cursed long and fluently as he glared at his mount. The animal stood awkwardly, favouring the right foreleg that had found its way into a gopher hole, and Belman felt fear grip his heart at the prospect before him should the leg be broken. Closer examination showed the injury to be a bad sprain and the man cursed with renewed vigour at the knowledge that he would be immobile for at least a couple of days. By that time Gabe Dance, Lush and Marks could be close enough to cause him problems.

He straightened up after examining the ugly-looking mustang, conscious of the weight of the cross, and the pain where it dug into the lower part of his back, and studied the terrain carefully. His humour was restored as he saw the steady incline that rose from the trail up to the timberline, the thick clumps of mesquite that afforded ample cover and the stream in the distance. On the other side of the trail a bald cliff face reflected the sun's rays, a mass of rock that curved away in the distance and ran east to link up with the outer ring of the Little Pueblos. He could hole up in safety on the timberline and at the same time command a good view almost back as far as the point where the cleft in the mountains joined the trail. If anyone followed from Rimrock he would see them.

Satisfied, he led the lame mustang to where the trail forded the shallow stream that ran down from the snowline, and keeping to the stream, turned back up valley, then up its narrow course and almost through the timber before climbing out of its icy waters. He led the animal to within about thirty yards of the timber's edge and leaving it ground-hitched, retraced his steps to set about removing any tell-tale sign. The heavy cross he carried with him: not for one moment was he prepared to let it out of his sight, even though its awkward size and weight had him struggling and panting.

Regaining the timber-line he built himself a fire, and after a meal removed the harness and opened it up to examine the cross greedily.

His mind slipped back to the old church of St Theresa just over the Mexican border where he had taken refuge years ago, with a bullet wound in his thigh. He had spent days staring up at the empty cradle that had held such a cross as this, and had heard the story of the cross that had been taken together with all the other valuables by renegade Spaniards. The valley of Deloros had amassed wealth throughout the years and the church of St Theresa had unlimited funds to draw upon, but generations of devout Catholics had resisted the temptation to buy or make a new cross. They believed that in fullness of time, the old cross would be restored to them and would bring with it special benedictions.

If Belman were any judge, this cross would just about fit that cradle, and it that were so, he would be sure of infinitely more reward from the people of Deloros than he could obtain by cutting and selling gold and stones separately.

Only by dint of physical effort did he finally tear his gaze away and cover the cross over. As he smoked, he let his mind run on to the life he planned for himself back East. If a few more men had to die before he reached Deloros, then they would die and no matter.

From then until sundown, he sat at the edge of the timber, his eyes quartering the terrain, and after sundown he remained, dozing quietly, sure in the knowledge that he would pick up the noise of horsemen upon the trail below.

Long before the sun came up he had eaten and resumed his place at the edge of the timber. His inspection of his mustang revealed a more severe strain than he had at first suspected, and he reckoned it would take a week before the animal could fork his weight. A week was a long time for a man to kick his heels when a fortune awaited him, and Belman's mood spelt danger for anyone forking a bronc within range of his guns.

The morning dragged by with the heat haze shifting and shimmering, but apart from a small herd of buffalo that stopped briefly at the stream, nothing moved. He ate a cold lunch as he was not prepared to take the chance of a fire giving his presence away, and instead of risking a cigarette he bit off a length of the scented tobacco he favoured.

It was just after he had watered his horse and moved the animal to another spot where it could forage, that he saw the moving dots in the distance that were in fact Bellamy, Juarez, the Irish boy and girl and the led horses. The haze moved back over them for a while but when they re-emerged, they stayed except for when folds in the terrain hid them. A couple of hours later, when the trail's devious route brought them very little nearer he was still unable to identify the riders, then out of the haze more riders materialized, with two led horses.

Belman's face clouded. Two sets of riders so close together could mean the law. He had hoped to leave Dance to the mercy of the law, but it seemed the plan had not worked out.

It was late afternoon by the time the first bunch of riders were within recognizable distance. Clint and Mex he did not know but the two youngsters he knew to be members of the wagon train. The line of led horses interested him, then his attention was drawn to the rangy black with the wide, white blaze and the white left foreleg that the girl rode. That animal had belonged to Pat Lush. His eyes ranged the other horses and he was able to pick out Holt's bay and Con Mark's big, barrel-chested brown. Belman returned his attention to Clint and Mex, and even at the considerable distance he found them a bit too uncompromising for his liking. If they were lawmen, then they were deadly, un-relenting lawmen. He hoped he had made a good job of covering his tracks.

The horses had the scent of water in their nostrils and wanted to move faster, but the riders out front kept the pace down as they eyed the trail and glanced along the rising ground to the timberline. They passed along the trail below him and where he had led his horse into the stream they spent a lot of time.

Belman almost held his breath as he watched them and his hand was closed over his Winchester repeater for a long time before the group below resumed their places in the saddles and moved on downtrail. He watched them for a long time before turning his attention to the other two riders who were still a long way off. It took an hour for them to get close enough for recognition and at the same moment as Belman named them as Reardon and Kelly, he evolved his plan of campaign.

Hurrying to his horse he slipped its picketing rope and drove it deeper into the timber. Returning, he undid his saddle-roll and pulled out the garb he had worn as Father Dewar. After effecting the necessary change and struggling into the harness that held the cross, he picked up his saddle-roll, saddle and harness and made his way down to the trail.

He squatted alongside the trail and waited the last few minutes before the two Irishmen topped the rise that hid them temporarily, composing his features into the benign sanctimonious lines the men knew. He noted also that they were riding horses that had belonged to Gabe Dance and Ike Holmes. He knew Holmes to be dead, but it was good to know Gabe Dance had no further need for his horse.

Belman stood up, welcome in every feature as the two men reined in and struggled with words of greeting.

'A fortuitous meeting, my sons,' he said unctuously. 'Although I never doubted someone would come my way.'

'Sure, Father, it's good to see you,' Reardon growled. 'We'd given you up for dead.'

Belman's eyebrows lifted. 'And why should you give me up for dead?' he asked.

'Well, it's a wild country and the time ran on,' Kelly put in. His eyes had strayed to the harness that held the cross and suddenly feeling completely deflated, he choked back the curse that came to his tongue.

'You forget I'm not a stranger to this country,' Belman replied easily. 'Mind, I intended to return to the wagon trail the same day, but I was led further away by a conviction that at the end of my journey I would recover the cross for your people.'

By now Reardon also had seen the cross and he stared in undisguised amazement.

'That conviction was right,' Belman continued. 'I saw those killers hiding it and when they had moved on enough I dug it up. I didn't get much luck finding my way back but you've found me instead.' He followed their glances at his saddle and smiled disarmingly. 'I took a tumble back up there,' he nodded towards the timber. 'My horse broke its neck and it looked as though I had a long walk in front of me but I knew someone would happen along.'

The Irishmen dropped to the ground and gripped Belman's hand in turn.

'We'll get you saddled up, Father,' said Reardon, reaching down for the saddle.

Belman placed a restraining hand on his arm. 'Those big horses of yours are more suited to you I think.' He would need something a lot better under him than those

89

clumsy animals in due course, so now was the right time to make the choice.

Reardon's face clouded, but looking into the wide-eyed innocence of the Father he forced a grin to his lips. 'Sure, Father, you ride this one.' He nodded towards the rangy bay that had carried Gabe Dance for the last few years.

'Thank you, my son.' Belman's voice dripped balm, and he stood aside as the two Irishmen fixed the saddles. He was just climbing into the saddle when he paused. 'Perhaps one of you would like to carry the cross for a while? It's been a long haul from up there.'

Reardon and Kelly nearly fell over themselves in their eagerness but Reardon got there first, and a couple of minutes later the ginger-haired giant stood in silent awe as he contemplated the solid weight of the cross.

'Holy Father!' he muttered. 'It must be worth a king's ransom.'

Belman affected not to hear and pointed to the stream.

'We'd better water these horses,' he said. 'Then it will be better if we head back up trail.'

There was a question in the other men's eyes, and he laughed easily.

'When coming on to this trail I realized I'd been this way before.' He paused to let the fact settle. 'And I remember now that about three miles back there's a fork that leads through the Pueblos to Portales and from Portales it's a pretty good trail down through Elida and across the Pecos to Roswell. We should reach El Paso before the wagon train.'

The others nodded although Reardon was hardly listening. He had the feel of the cross now and his mind was a whirl with the mad desire for possession. He was just two bullets away from a fortune, one bullet was easy. He could kill Kelly without batting an eyelid, but a man of the cloth... His mind shied away from it. The same problem beset Kelly. As they rode away from the stream to the fork in the trail an uneasy silence settled over them, a silence that told Belman its own story. He was lucky. When the time was ripe he could use two bullets without compunction. For the present he was content to have the two men along. It was conceivable that they would have their uses. When they reached the fork in the trail there was respect on Reardon's face.

'Your memory didn't tell no lies, Father,' he said. 'How far is it to the town you mentioned, Portales?'

Belman drew rein and pointed to the distant peaks of the Pueblo Twins. The haze had lifted temporarily and the two peaks stood out in bold relief. 'The trail runs clear across the shoulder of the mountain on the left then south-west to Portales. Say two

91

days steady riding.' Reardon stopped for a long time studying the terrain ahead. He was busy getting the picture right but when Belman continued, he had to reshape this thoughts. 'We lose sight of those peaks a few times and the going gets rough here and there, but once over the Pueblos it's easy going to Portales.'

They kept going steadily for a few hours until the horse Reardon rode showed signs of flagging, then Belman called a halt. They were stopped under an overhang of rock on the one side, with steeply rising ground on the other, and as the Irishmen prepared a meal, Belman climbed back into the saddle.

'I must commune awhile, my sons,' he murmured, his face seraphic, and the two men nodded. Ruffians though they were, their religion went deep, and the need of a priest to hold silent communion went un-questioned. Belman rode along the trail until it veered away from view, then branched off where the overhanging cliffs gave out in favour of gentle sloping grassland.

Judging his distance, he rode back along the hill until he was above and behind the Irishmen, then ground-hitching his horse, made his way quietly to the rocks immedi-ately above the trail. He squatted in a cleft that funnelled up the voices of the two men who fussed around the fire that sent a thick column of smoke aloft.

'He's the same as any other man,' Reardon snarled.

'You know that's not so, Jamie.' Kelly's reply was slow. 'Killing a man of the cloth will bring us nothing but bad luck.'

'And what if I kill him? Is that right by you?'

'No need to kill him, Jamie,' Kelly said after a long silence. 'Just leave him here. It's his own affair if he dies then.'

'That's right!' Reardon replied. 'He had no horse when we met him and all we'll be doing is leaving him the same way.'

Belman moved away from his vantage point carefully and returned to his mount, mulling over the situation. Reardon had told him what they had found at Rimrock and how the wagon train was in good hands. He also guessed from what he had been told about Bellamy and Juarez that they had put two and two together, and had trailed him out of Rimrock. As he swung into the saddle he hit upon the plan to divert suspicion away from himself, and to use the two Irishmen to achieve his ends.

'I think my purpose has been served with you good people,' Belman said quietly, having rejoined the Irishmen. 'The wagon train will have managed without my ministrations right to El Paso. They won't hurt any from there to California without me.' He paused, conscious of the hard looks on the faces of

93

the other two. 'If you think you can follow the trail to Portales, then I'll go about my business. Work waits for me to the west. Let nothing stop you from delivering the cross to your people.'

The breath hissed out of Reardon and Kelly. To have their problem solved so easily had them beaming with pleasure.

'Have no fear, Father. We'll find our way and we'll guard this cross with our lives,' Reardon bellowed.

Belman nodded, apparently satisfied, then a frown crossed his face. 'I should keep it out of the hands of those two men you told me about, Bellamy and Juarez. They'll be catching up with you eventually.' He could picture them back-tracking when the trail they followed continued to show nothing, and they would not miss the arrival and departure at the stream of four more horses.

'Leave it to us, Father. No-one but me and Kelly are going to lay a hand on it.'

Belman ate a good meal and when the others started cleaning up, he took his leave. They watched him go until the trail was hidden behind a bluff, and when they judged he was far enough away, their excitement bubbled in unrestrained laughter. Sobering thoughts and greed eventually stayed their hilarity and soon they were eyeing each other with guarded reserve.

Belman obliterated his tracks when he

moved off the trail and he rode from cover to cover, up and ever up, to where he could keep the trail under constant surveillance. If Reardon and Kelly told their tales right, then any suspicion of Father Dewar would be allayed. The two immigrants might even be left alone to find their own way back to the wagon train in which case, he, Belman, could retake the cross wherever and whenever he liked. He permitted himself a broad smile of satisfaction at the way things were working out.

CHAPTER SEVEN

'I'd say we've been fooled some, Clint,' Mex spoke slowly as he returned from a scouting foray. Clint handed him a mug of coffee, and grinned back good-humouredly.

'Get outside of that and you'll feel better. I reckon if we back-track we'll soon find where the bluff was pulled.'

Mex took the mug of coffee and savoured its aroma for a few moments. He cast a quizzical eye at Matt Sullivan and the girl. 'How are you two making out? Any objections to retracing our steps?'

'No, sir,' Matt replied quickly. 'Anything you say will suit us.' The girl nodded, a smile on her lips.

'If we take the trail I'm guessing to have to follow, it'll likely stretch the time by another week at least before we can join up with the wagon train,' Mex continued.

The two youngsters nodded their understanding and the pards exchanged satisfied glances. The young immigrants were settling down admirably and far from being a hindrance, they were taking a share of the chores.

They got under way quickly, and with Mex

out in front moved back along the trail. The Mexican did not stop until they arrived at the point where they had forded the stream. He dismounted, and handed the reins over to Matt. 'Let 'em take their fill a bit further down,' he said, nodding downtrail. 'There's plenty to look at here.'

Clint joined him and together they studied the banks of the stream. They poked around in silence for a long time, then both sat back on their hunkers.

'I'd say three of the four cayuses that have taken water since we were here were ridden, the other was led.' Clint lit a smoke as he spoke, and Mex searched for a cheroot as he replied.

'I'd agree to that, Clint, and those cayuses were the ones we left to Reardon and Kelly back at Rimrock.' Clint nodded his agreement as Mex continued. 'So either they've come from Rimrock with another *hombre,* or the third feller joined 'em pretty close to here, and considering it's here we lost the trail, I'd say the feller we trailed joined up with 'em hereabouts.'

What Mex said made good sense and after they had refilled all water containers, they set off in pursuit of the horsemen who had watered their horses earlier. Clint and Mex exchanged knowing nods when they came to where Belman had met up with Reardon and Kelly. They picked up the tracks where

98

the trail forked, and turned due west on the long haul to Portales.

They stopped for a meal where Belman, Kelly and Reardon had stopped, and shortly afterwards discovered they were following three horses not four.

'That *hombre* sure knows how to cover his tracks when he slides off,' Mex grumbled. He scanned the ridges on each side of the trail as he spoke, but he sensed no particular danger lurked there.

'Looks like he borrowed a cayuse, then pushed off when he got fed up with the company.' Clint rubbed his chin reflectively.

Mex shook his head. 'Nope, there's a mite more to it,' he said. 'If he'd just wanted to get adrift of 'em he'd have upped the speed but still kept to the trail.'

'I guess you're right, and that means we'll have to keep our eyes peeled for him.'

'Could be,' Mex agreed. 'But he's already let us pass him by once. Why didn't he try a cayuse from us? He must have had Reardon and Kelly in view at the same time and opined he'd do better with them.'

'Huh, we'll just have to watch out for him,' Clint remarked. 'Maybe we'll find out something about him when we catch up with those other *hombres*.'

They relapsed into silence as the trail funnelled into a deep canyon, and both men studied the craggy walls with great care. The man they had followed out of Rimrock knew he was being trailed. The degree of their danger depended upon just how much the fact mattered to him.

Canyon followed canyon, until late in the evening, the terrain opened out and spread in ever-rising folds to a ridge that hid the long downhill run to Portales. The sun was just about to edge behind the Pueblo Twins when just ahead of them, two horsemen and a led horse emerged out of a depression, heading into the sun. Kelly and Reardon were unmistakable. They sat their mounts like sacks of grain. Bellamy and Juarez exchanged contented glances. They would shortly be in a position to satisfy their curiosity concerning the lone rider.

Kelly and Reardon became less and less communicative as the miles rolled slowly under the cumbersome hooves of the draught horses. Reardon, with the weight of the cross dragging at his shoulders, could only think of its weight in terms of value. He felt almost physical pain at the thought of division by two. Kelly could almost see his mind ticking over whenever Reardon eased the position of the harness. He had given up offering to take over the burden. Reardon's last refusal had been explosive and accompanied by a look that held the menace of death in it.

For hours, each man had studiously avoided riding ahead of the other. Reardon's ability with a rifle worried Kelly, whilst thoughts of the long knife that hung in its scabbard on Kelly's belt kept lining Reardon's back with goose pimples. The chill hand of death fought with greed and the excitement of possession.

'How are you going to set about selling that hunk of gold, Jamie?' Kelly asked at long last.

Reardon stared across at him and deep lines furrowed his brow. He supposed gold was gold anywhere, but this was a strange country, and he could well run into trouble trying to trade his prize. The more he thought about it, only one way seemed sensible.

'Get it cut up and trade it in small pieces,' he grunted.

There was a bleak look in Kelly's eyes when he posed his next question.

'Why not get it carved up and shared out right now then?'

'We'll share out soon enough,' snarled Reardon, ignoring the menace in the other man's question. 'Let's get under cover some place so that we can't get the job done clean without losing half of it in dust. We'll get a room in Portales and take our time over it.'

It seemed like a good idea and Kelly appeared somewhat mollified, but Reardon's brow blackened at the bare prospect of carving the cross up two ways and his hand moved around to the butt of his rifle instinctively. He sensed Kelly's eyes on him and he jerked his head towards the rolling slopes on the side of the trail.

'Looked to me like a hare just to the left of that big bush,' he said easing the rifle into his hand. 'Keep a look-out. We need all the red meat we can find.'

Kelly's suspicions were allayed to some extent and food being a subject that could capture his attention at any time, he found himself thinking of roast hare to the exclusion of all else. Coming up to the top of a ridge he forgot his suspicions to such an extent that his mount was a length in front of Reardon. He owed his life to the last all-embracing glance Reardon flashed around before pulling the trigger. Reardon's mumbled curse brought Kelly's head around fast and the man took in the position of the rifle barrel, still held rock-like in Reardon's hands and not far behind them the four riders and string of led horses.

Kelly understood Reardon's rage. To be thwarted in the last second must have been a powerful disappointment. Kelly hauled his mount around and stared deep into Reardon's bloodshot eyes. 'So ... that's how it is.' His voice was quiet, sibilant, and Reardon shivered a little as a premonition of the run of cold steel into his vitals flitted through his mind.

'Wh – what do you mean?' he stammered.

'You were all set to blast off that gun into my back.'

There was no trace of temper in Kelly's voice and for that reason alone Reardon shivered again. A blustering Kelly was something he could handle, but a quiet, controlled Kelly was a revelation to him, a bitter revelation.

'And why would I do that?' he croaked.

'Just so you could hang on to that cross yourself, Jamie, that's why.' A slow mocking smile crossed Kelly's dark face. 'You'll never get another chance, Jamie, never.'

The two men were still glaring balefully at each other when Mex Juarez topped the ridge. There was a decided lack of cordiality in their reply to the Mexican's greeting, and when Clint, Matt Sullivan and Kathy Mullins gathered around there was no change in their manner.

'So you found it, eh?' Clint came straight to the point, and leaning over in the saddle, patted the weather-worn casing of the cross.

'Yeah, we found it,' snapped back Reardon. 'So what!?'

'So we escort you back safely to where you and the cross belong,' Mex said quietly. The expressions of pain on the faces of the Irish men brought a fleeting smile to his lips.

'We don't need you along. We'll find our own way.' The way Kelly said it, Reardon found himself thinking that perhaps he would like company after all.

'How come you've got the cross?' Clint had suddenly lost his easy-going look, and his face was hard. 'You *hombres* never found it in Rimrock. Did you kill that feller who begged a cayuse from you, because he was toting that cross.'

'No! No!' shouted Reardon. 'He gave it to us.'

The hard stares of Bellamy and Juarez made him doubt the fact himself and he rushed to explain. 'It was Father Dewar, he followed the thieves and saw them hiding the cross then lost his way. His horse got killed not far from where we met him. He said he had work elsewhere and asked us to take the cross back.'

At the mention of Father Dewar excited exclamations came from Kathy Mullins and Matt Sullivan, but Clint and Mex did not seem to share their enthusiasm. An element of doubt started to creep into their minds however. As they understood things, when Dewar had left the wagon train, the intended route had been via Santa Fe. He had certainly kept going in that direction. Then the same thought crossed their minds. They had trailed him out of Rimrock, and whoever had been in Rimrock, he'd had his hands in blood up to the elbows. If he had passed on the cross to Reardon and Kelly, then he was using them for his own purpose.

'We were told not to let the cross out of our hands,' Kelly said meaningly.

'I guess we'll not quarrel with that,' Clint replied. 'You'll need a lot of help holding on to it though when you hit some towns between here and El Paso.'

'We'll take care of any trouble that comes along,' insisted Kelly but both Clint and Mex shook their heads.

'That cross isn't just your affair,' Mex said. His handsome face held authority and Kelly had trouble meeting his gaze. 'Everybody in the wagon train has got some interest in it, and we'll see it's returned. Now get moving uptrail, and we'll make camp some place over that ridge.'

With bad grace the two giant Irishmen set their mounts to the rise, but now at least they were able to ride in safety. Neither man was particularly bright, and plotting their way around the protection of Bellamy and Juarez was hard work. They struggled with the problem in silence until Mex called a halt for the night, and neither was near to a solution. Belman, who had witnessed the joining of forces, had no trouble with his plans though. He reckoned upon a steady rate of liquidation as greed turned to treachery. Long before El Paso he expected to find maybe just one man and the girl between him and a fortune. Girls were two a penny back east with a fortune in your pocket, so he'd likely save himself a lot of trouble if he put a bullet through her same as he would kill a man. When it was obvious that they were making camp, Belman turned to the north and rode for an hour before resting for the night.

The one flaw in Belman's plan jerked him out of near sleep into a sitting position, with cold sweat standing out on his forehead. He suddenly realized he had no guarantee that Reardon and Kelly would not cut up the cross and share out. The thought persisted and he had to struggle against the desire to head straight for their camp. If it were only the Irishmen he would have given way to the impulse, but Bellamy and Juarez presented problems. The night passed with Belman's mind a torment of doubt and rage at his own stupidity, and when Clint and Mex broke camp the next morning he was watching from a position he had taken up an hour before dawn. When he saw the harness in place on Reardon's broad shoulders, he heaved a sigh of relief and headed for Portales.

'Well, there's Portales!'

Mex held his pinto on the top of a ridge and pointed to the bustling cattle town that nestled beneath the hill.

As they watched, a stage coach emerged

far to the south out of the heat haze and its own dust, heading for Portales, and tiny moving dots that were horsemen streamed in and out of town. Bunches of cattle were grouped along the ribbon of river that reflected back the late afternoon sun, and here and there a lone puncher showed near to a group of cattle. Altogether, it was a contrasting scene of quiet and movement.

They entered Portales from the south as the sun slid down over the Pueblos, and on both sides of the dusty road people stopped to stare at them. The long string of led horses was excuse enough to stare but the strange garb of the three Irishmen had the townsfolk pop-eyed with amazement, and the dark beauty of Kathy Mullins had many a man licking his lips. There was something about the Mexican and his rugged companion at the head of the little cavalcade that stifled any ribald comments, and the men along the sidewalks watched in silence as the Mexican pulled his pinto to a halt outside the most solid-looking building in town, the gaol-house.

A tall, square man, sporting a large moustache, with a sheriff's badge upon his faded shirt, pushed himself away from the door-frame and came to the sidewalk rail. His face was set in hard lines as he studied first Mex then Clint.

'You *hombres* have sure come to the right

place,' he said smoothly. 'Saved me the chore of looking for you.'

'How come?' Clint asked slowly.

'I was all set to come and round you up,' the sheriff replied blandly. 'Heard you were mixed up in killing some folk from a wagon train just south of Amarillo, an' that you were in my territory.'

The crowd alongside the sheriff increased as men moved up along the sidewalk to satisfy their curiosity.

'That's not true!' shouted Matt Sullivan indignantly. 'They had nothing to do with what happened to the wagon train.'

The sheriff gave Matt a pitying glance. 'They maybe bluffed you, son,' he replied. 'But Father Dewar sure had 'em to rights. He says they joined up with that Dance feller and his gang then headed back for the wagon train. I guess they were gonna take the settlers by a different route than Dance had taken so's to take off the heat, then rejoin Dance later.'

Neither Clint nor Mex made any contribution to the conversation but Matt went to expostulate again then appeared to think better of it. He tilted his bowler hat back on his head and scratched the thick mop of ginger hair doubtfully. The sheriff could be right. How did he know whether or not they were members of the Dance gang? They had started the wagon train off on a different tack and they had left to look for Gabe Dance and his men. What did he know about them? And how did he know that they were not even now plotting to take the cross as and when it suited their purpose.

Until this moment Matt had not given much thought to the intrinsic value of the cross, but now he realized the full import of its worth, and his attention switched immediately to big Jamie Reardon who sat his saddle in painful awareness of its value. The need to take possession and preserve it for his kinfolk flooded his mind so that he failed to notice Mex and Clint dismount and walk into the gaol-house ahead of the sheriff. He determined then and there to take charge of it at the first opportunity.

A deputy stepped down to the dirt-road and came alongside Reardon. 'You'd better take those cayuses to the livery on the edge of town.' He nodded towards the north end of Main Street. 'I guess Luke will turn 'em loose for you in the open paddock, then I'll see to fixing you up with some place to stay until we get the lowdown on these two *hombres.*'

Lew Mallin, the deputy, could see by the wide grins of some Portales folk that left to fend for themselves, the Irish immigrants would have to run the gauntlet of a lot of backchat that could end up in trouble, so like the good law officer he was, he spread himself to prevent the trouble brewing. Reardon nodded his thanks and kicked his horse's flanks to get it moving again. The others followed in his wake and the crowd contented themselves with remarks to each other. When the Irish folk left the livery stable, Mallin was right on hand to take them to the Lone Trail Hotel. He saw them settled in, and fixed up for a meal to be prepared for the girl before returning to the gaol-house.

On the opposite side of the street Belman stood at the window of the coach-builder's store, and watched the deputy leave the hotel. A tight smile played on his lips as he turned to watch Zach Tranter hammer a strip of metal along the length of the wooden cross he had fashioned.

'It's gonna make this thing kinda heavy to tote around,' Tranter grunted as he hammered some rivets home. 'Still I guess you know your business best.'

'We all have to carry some burden,' Belman replied sanctimoniously. Tranter was unimpressed. So long as the holy man paid up for the hunk of redwood that now resembled a cross, then he could tote it to hell and gone for all he, Tranter cared. He spat a long stream of tobacco juice into a cuspidor and stared at his handiwork, now completed.

'Waal, I reckon you've sure got yourself enough of a burden here, mister. Anyway it's done if you want to take it.'

Belman picked it up, weighing it in his

hands thoughtfully.

'You've made a good job of it.' He placed a couple of coins on to the work bench. 'I'll collect it later. After I've made a couple of calls.'

'Suit yourself,' Tranter replied, eyeing the coins in a satisfied manner. 'I'll be working for another hour or so.'

Belman smiled and crossed to the door. He looked up and down, then slipped out on to the sidewalk. In half-an-hour it would be dark and he could remove the cross without drawing too much attention to himself. He grinned as he saw the pinto and dun gelding tethered to the hitch-rail in front of the gaol-house. With luck, Bellamy and Juarez would be out of action for a long time to come.

Inside the sheriff's office, Luke Daley sifted through the pile of articles Mex had unwrapped from his saddle-roll. He had heard their story and it seemed most convincing. Daley, being a fair judge of men, took them for straight shooters. Still, a man could be wrong, and he had the word of a priest that they were mixed up with a gang of killers.

'How come you're so durned interested in recovering the stolen property for the immigrants?' Daley asked. 'You not being law-men, it seems a bit odd to set off hunting a gang of killers on account of a wagon train of strangers.'

'Yeah, you'd maybe think it's strange,' Mex

replied lazily. 'But I guess we've got pride enough in the West to want to convince folk that most Westerners can be trusted.'

There was some scepticism in the sheriff's eyes as he considered the Mexican's remark. 'Most lawmen have got the same notions, but they get staked every month for thinking that way,' he said. 'It don't add up when a couple of *hombres* do peace officers' work for nothing.'

Clint sighed, slowly and exasperatedly. 'Maybe we've got all the stake we want,' he grunted. 'And instead of talking you'd do better following up a few things that'll put us in the clear.'

'Like what?' Daley eased back in his chair and surveyed them.

'Like getting telegraphs to Abe Ferris, sheriff of Brush County, and Jed Delahay, sheriff of Butte, Montana. That's for a start. A couple of U.S. Marshals would be more than willing to vouch for us.'

'Abe Ferris I know,' Daley said quickly, and the suspicion had almost left his eyes. 'Can't say I've met Jed Delahay but I've heard of him plenty. If they'll vouch for you then I'd reckon that priest made a mistake. We're on the telegraph from the staging depot but you'll have to cool your heels in the pokey until I get replied.'

'Suits us so long as you see those mustangs out front get bedded down mighty soon,' Mex said, and Clint shrugged his wide shoulders philosophically.

'Sure thing, can't say I've ever let a cayuse suffer on account of its owner being no good.' Daley saw the glitter spring into the Mexican's eyes and had the good grace to grin. 'That's not saying the line of reasoning follows in this case.' He nodded his head towards the cells and resignedly, the two pards lined up to move in peacefully. Clint paused in the act of going through.

'Just one thing, Sheriff. Decent folk might get hurt if we spend too much time in your hoosegow.' Daley did not appear to take offence and Clint continued, 'Just see that young girl comes to no harm.'

'Nobody's gonna harm her in my territory, mister,' the sheriff answered stiffly. 'I've got a deputy looking out for the greenhorns right now.'

Satisfied, Clint and Mex allowed themselves to be directed into a cell and without ado, sat down on the hard bunks to enjoy a smoke. Daley slammed the gate shut and took his time over locking up.

'I'll see to getting some chow along,' he remarked as he turned away. The pards merely grunted in reply and the sheriff made his way through to the outer office. A couple of minutes later he slammed out of the gaol-house and made his way to the staging-depot.

CHAPTER EIGHT

Kathy Mullins felt a sense of well-being that had been absent for some time. Completely refreshed after a bath that had been laid on for her, she hurried to the room where a meal was to be sent up. A spasm of annoyance swept across her face as Jamie Reardon appeared from a doorway. She noticed he still wore the cross harness and had not bothered to remove any trail dust. His bulk loomed in front of her and she came to a stop.

'You and me, Kathy, we could have some fun together.' His pig eyes were alight with desire and he leaned close to her, his hot breath on her cheeks. 'I wouldn't share this with anyone else,' he said indicating the load on his back, 'but you now, I'd set you up like a lady just so long as you'd be nice to me.'

'Get out of my way, Jamie Reardon!' Kathy stormed. 'I want nothing to do with you now or ever.'

Reardon reached down and before Kathy could stop him he crushed her to him. His massive hands held her like a vice and his bewhiskered lips found hers in a long savage kiss. She hated herself as his hard virile body sent its message pounding through her veins and had its answer deep down in her stomach. When he let her go she found it hard to pull away, and when he stood aside for her to rush past he laughed tersely. He'd get her yet, and when he did, she would have no use for lesser men like Matt Sullivan. He lumbered back into the room he had been allotted with Kelly and sat on the edge of a bed. The hard metal of the cross chafed his backbone and he eased his arms out of the harness. He pursed his lips as he considered what to do with the cross. Kelly had already gone to slake his alkali-lined throat with the hard stuff, but Reardon was not prepared to leave the cross where other men could find it. The problem passed from him all too soon.

A noise at the door brought his head up and he had difficulty in mustering a smile for the benign-looking Father Dewar who stood just inside the door dressed in a long black habit.

'I got to thinking you may have trouble getting that cross back to where it belongs, Jamie,' he said, closing the door and bringing the wooden cross into view. 'So I decided to help you.'

Reardon looked at the cross a couple of times unable to comprehend the purport of things. 'How are you going to help?' he asked.

'Well, if you substitute this one for the real

thing and head straight along the stage route south, you'll give yourself a couple of days lead before they discover the truth. Y'know I don't trust that Bellamy and Juarez and I'd feel happier if you had the cross under your sole control.'

Reardon's eyes gleamed with excitement.

'Now that's not a bad idea, Father.' He eyed the wooden cross carefully, noting the strip metal running along its length. 'You've got a good memory for size too. I'd say that'll fit this carrier like a glove.'

Belman smiled indulgently.

'Try it,' he said quietly and Reardon crossed to the door, turned the key and returned to the bed.

Quickly he unfastened the studs of the heavy-duty cover and uncovered the cross. The metal reflected dully the light from the kerosene lamp on the table but the ruby and diamonds glistened where the light touched them. Briefly Reardon drooled over its fabulous beauty and he thrust it under a bed and picking up the wooden one, fitted it into the cover, then fastening the studs turned to Belman, his face beaming.

The smile froze on his face as he saw the long knife in Belman's hand. His eyes switched to the pseudo priest's face and the savagery there made him gibber with fright. His vocal chords seemed paralysed and his mouth worked frantically but emitted no

117

sound. As Belman slid forward Reardon tried to pull himself together, but he was too late. He gulped as the run of cold steel ended in his heart. Belman watched him without a flicker of remorse as his knees buckled, and gave his huge bulk a contemptuous push, spread-eagling him on the bed on top of the imitation cross.

Casually Belman recovered the cross from under the bed, and drawing it under the cover of his habit, unlocked the door and left by the window on the veranda. The night was black and the end of the veranda, levelling with the corner of the hotel, was in the deepest shadow. Belman waited until no-one was near to see him descend to the sidewalk, then he climbed down.

He had timed things very neatly. He knew Sullivan to be in the chop-house finishing his meal and Kelly was down in the Lone Puncher saloon drinking a brand of rye that had a kick like a mule. Pretty soon one or the other would be looking for Reardon, and with luck, one of them would get stuck for the murder.

He left the cross just below the livery stable when he went in to collect his horse, and after dickering with Lew Smart for a second string cayuse, he left the livery and retrieved it. Back in his hotel at the north end of Main Street, he paid the sleepy-eyed oldster at the desk and it took him no more than five minutes to collect his gear before heading out of Portales for keeps.

Belman had no sooner passed out of earshot of Portales than his plan came to fruition. Simultaneous with young Matt returning from the chop-house, Sheriff Luke Daley pushed his way into the Lone Puncher saloon where Kelly, almost drunk, was busy battering an inoffensive-looking storekeeper who had made some remark about his bowler hat. As Eli Whitton went down again Daley stalked up to the rampaging Irishman. He jabbed the muzzle of his .45 into Kelly's midriff and glared bleakly at him.

'That's enough, feller,' he gritted as Whitton sat on his haunches and dabbed at his bruised jaw with a dirty handkerchief. 'Now get going! I'll take you back to your quarters to cool off.'

Kelly stared at the sheriff owlishly for a while and tried shifting away from the disconcerting ring of steel digging into his navel. Daley jabbed harder.

'Next time you cool off in a cell, so get going!' he ordered.

Kelly lumbered out with Daley following him close and as the batwing doors swung behind them the customers of the Lone Puncher saloon roared with laughter. Eli Whitton eyed them balefully and staggered to the bar for enough rye to take the pain away.

When Matt Sullivan knocked tentatively at Kathy Mullins' door, he thought he heard the sounds of sobbing. A full minute went by before the door opened a fraction and he could tell by the girl's red-rimmed eyes that he had heard aright. She opened the door wider and he entered quickly. With his arms around her he looked earnestly into her face.

'What's wrong, Kathy?' he said. 'What's happened?'

The girl forced a smile and shook her head. 'Nothing, Matt, nothing,' she replied.

'You don't cry for nothing, Kathy,' he reasoned. 'Tell me what's wrong.'

As his eyes searched her face he saw the raw skin around her mouth where Reardon's coarse beard had rubbed, and the grip marks from Reardon's dirty hands on the sleeves of her white blouse. The rage welled up in him as he worked things out for himself.

'Jamie Reardon's been bothering you, Kathy, hasn't he?'

Kathy did not answer and Matt held her away from him, searching her face. She made no attempt to deny the fact and he knew he was right. He let her go and turned abruptly for the door.

'I'll kill him!' he raged. 'I'll kill him!'

Kathy reached forward for him and held on. Her face reflecting the fear she felt for young Matt.

'No, Matt, no!' she cried. 'Leave him be! He kissed me when I couldn't stop him, that's all.'

'Stay here, Kathy,' he ordered. 'I'll show Jamie Reardon I've grown up. He won't try kissing my girl again.'

He slammed the door behind him leaving Kathy with a feeling of dismay. She knew that some day soon Matt would be the equal of any man, but right now Jamie Reardon seemed a mite too much for him. She dreaded to think what Matt would look like when he returned.

Matt lost no time and ran along the corridor to Reardon's room. He heard voices down below on the stairs as he pushed the door open and thrust his way into the room. He came to a stop with a gasp as he saw Reardon's bulk spread-eagled on the bed, with the knife handle sticking out of the crimsoned flannel shirt.

'Oh no, Kathy! No!' he exclaimed in horror, then without being aware of his action, he took hold of the knife as though taking it would bring Reardon back to life. Belman had struck well however, and the knife stayed firm.

The door opened as footsteps stopped in the corridor and Matt half-turned to see Kelly's bloated face and the level, grey eyes of Sheriff Daley surveying him. Daley pushed Kelly to one side and came in closer, his gun pointed unwaveringly to Matt's heart.

'Stand aside,' he ordered, and with his mind in a torment, Matt did as he was told.

Daley surveyed Reardon's unsavoury corpse with almost clinical interest, and reaching over, felt the pulse, then felt the still warm flesh of the face before giving his full attention to Matt.

'You did a good job of it, youngster,' he said slowly. 'I guess you wanted to kill him that bad you won't mind taking your punishment.'

Matt said nothing. His mouth seemed tongue-tied anyway, but to make it worse Kathy was at the door taking in the scene. He waited for her to explain to the hard-eyed sheriff but she said nothing. She just stood in the doorway staring wild-eyed, petrified. Kelly sobered suddenly and leaned forward to stare as though hypnotized at the knife.

'My God, Jamie!' he exclaimed, then as he turned to look at Matt Sullivan he checked the words that flowed to his lips. No point in drawing attention to the cross. The only explanation that sprung to Kelly's mind for the murder of Reardon, was that Sullivan wanted the cross for himself.

'C'mon move!' Daley said at length, and Matt walked through the door in a dream. He kept his eyes away from Kathy who shrunk away from him as he passed.

'You'd best go back to your room, ma'am,' Daley said gently as he drew alongside the girl. 'It's no sight for a lady.'

He prodded his gun into Matt's back and made for the stairs while Kathy rushed back to her room, her world completely shattered. Never for one moment had she thought that Matt would kill, not even in a fit of temper, but she had been wrong. Her lover was a killer, had used cold steel into the bargain. Her father was dead, her lover on the way to whatever punishment they meted out to killers in the West, and Bellamy and Juarez were in prison. Her future looked bleak. There was only Kelly left, and he would be harder to fight off then Reardon once set upon taking her. For a brief despairing moment she was ready to give in, and in the need for human company, go to meet anything that Kelly might demand.

Her pride held her, but when a meal was brought up to her, she ignored it despite her gnawing hunger, and throwing herself on the bed sobbed herself dry of emotion.

Clint and Mex were drinking their second mug of coffee after the excellent meal Lew Mallin had brought them when Daley entered the cell block, pushing Matt Sullivan along before him. The pards stood up and watched in surprise as Daley stopped at the next cell to theirs and ordered Matt inside. The sheriff slammed the gate shut behind the young Irishman and turned the key in the lock. He was about to return to the outer office when Clint spoke.

'What in tarnation have you brought him in for?' he asked, his rugged face set in hard lines.

Daley stared back at him coolly. 'If you two *hombres* are anything like the company you keep, I don't place much store on hearing anything favourable about you from Ferris or Delahay.'

'Stop talking in riddles, man and tell us what he's done,' Mex put in smoothly.

Daley shrugged and bit off a chew of tobacco before replying.

'He knifed a man to death. The big red-haired *hombre* he says was called Reardon.' Daley paused and looked meaningly at his prisoners. 'And there's nothing anyone's gonna do to prove otherwise, because I caught the *hombre* with his hand on the knife.'

'Suppose you tell us what happened, Matt,' Clint called out.

'It's not going to matter much what I say,' Matt replied thickly. 'The sheriff saw me with my hand on the knife like he says, so what is there for me to say?'

Matt's reply failed to satisfy the pards and Mex tried the direct approach.

'Why did you kill him then?' he called out and the denial came quickly before Matt could reason things out.

'I didn't kill him. I couldn't kill anyone that way.'

Relief showed in the faces of the two men. No matter which way it looked they would back the youngster if he were innocent.

'What about Kelly?' Clint called out. 'Where was he?'

'He couldn't have done it. He was drinking down in a saloon and the sheriff brought him up drunk.' Matt did not want the pards to develop the line of questioning. He would resist the temptation to save his skin by telling the world his girl had killed in defence of her honour. He would have to wait until she came forward to clear him.

A couple of hours later he received a jolt that sent terror into his heart and fury into his mind. Daley came in and stopped outside his cell.

'I've been talking to the young lady, Miss Mullins,' the sheriff said. 'I guess I had to drag the truth out of her but she said you left her saying you were going to kill Reardon, and she followed you down shortly afterwards which was when I arrived.' He let this sink in then continued in a more kindly manner. 'If there's anything you'd like then say so, because you haven't got long to satisfy your fancy.'

When Matt said nothing, Daley turned on his heel and left the cell-block, shaking his head in sorrow.

Matt Sullivan was stunned. That Kathy could kill at all was a shock; that she could allow another to pay the penalty was almost unbelievable. The affair defied reason. One word from her would have freed him and no court would have convicted her. A woman's honour was something that mattered out West, that much he knew. His mind made mad circles around the problem until he fell asleep from pure exhaustion.

Neither Kathy Mullins nor Kelly slept that night. The girl tossed and turned in her bed in a fever of anxiety. Her future was so insecure that the doubts and horrors crowded in and through everything Matt's face was there. Although she wanted nothing more to do with him, she almost cried aloud at the prospect of him forfeiting his life for his crime, and she blamed herself for having allowed him to see her distressed after her brush with Reardon. Better to have allowed Reardon to have his way with her if this could have been averted but it was too late for recrimination. Reardon was dead and Matt was a murderer.

Kelly rode through the night with a growing fear in his mind. When he first cleared Portales his jubilation ran high. The fortune bruising his backbone was welcome pain and his thoughts ran on to a life of ease in which strong drink and weak-willed women played a major part. But with the solitude, the glowering cliffs abutting the trail eerily echoing the steady hoofbeats of his horse, and the shadows that a pale moon cast across his path, he began to feel that a thousand eyes were watching him, and forces were gathering to take his prize away.

The canyon was long and the echoing tattoo of hoofbeats became more insistent, and Kelly was afraid. His mouth parted wide with apprehension, and terror was in his eyes. He uttered a gasp of relief when his mount cleared the canyon and raced along open country, but the relief was short-lived. He saw phantoms in the shadows beyond the trail where the moonlight failed to reach. A coyote howled three times and a mountain lion roared. Normally gregarious, Kelly was finding solitude hard to bear.

When he started the run into another long canyon one pair of eyes watched him. Belman, hearing the rapid hoofbeats long before horse and rider drew abreast and swept on, had pulled off the trail and waited to see who was following so fast. The moon was straight above and he had no difficulty in recognizing Kelly. His lip curled contemptuously at the abject terror on Kelly's face, then stretched to a smile as he saw the fake cross in the harness upon the man's back. He reckoned Kelly had the heck of a shock coming to him. The cross wouldn't fetch enough *dinero* to pay for liniment to ease the bruises his burden had caused.

'I guess we can't all win,' Belman said aloud when the hoofbeats of Kelly's horse had died away. He leaned over and patted the bulky bundle that was fixed across the saddle of his pack horse and a deep contentment flowed through him. Things had certainly worked out. His self-congratulation gave way to caution as he considered the speed of Kelly's departure. It could be that the man was being followed closely, so he upped the speed until clearing the canyon. Elida was the next township on the southern trail, and he decided to enter it from the south. The long, black, priest's habit once more reposed in his saddle-roll and Belman looked what he really was, a hard, cold, murderous gunman.

CHAPTER NINE

It was a couple of hours after sunup when Luke Daley went into the staging depot. Cy Coles, the night-duty man was just enjoying a mug of java that gave a tang to the musty air. He stood up when Daley entered and poured him a mug from the simmering pot. He nodded towards two forms on his desk.

'That's what you want, Luke,' he said.

Daley grasped the mug of coffee eagerly enough, and taking a tentative sip the sheriff pulled the forms forward on the desk and sat down. Coles moved to the window while Daley studied the replies from Abe Ferris and Jed Delahay.

'Sure some recommendation.' Daley grunted at length.

Cy Coles turned from the window and nodded. 'Yeah, they rate mighty high, Luke. Done a lot of lawman's work for free. Delahay says they're Randall-Houston men an' that's the millionaire outfit of Butte, Montana. All the hands are on a percentage, and that covers gold and silver mines, so I guess they're not worried any about *dinero*.'

Daley turned to his coffee and drank deep before replying.

'Sure explains why they take time out to help folk,' he said. 'They struck me as straight shooters anyway. I guess they could be mighty mean at a pinch, but I couldn't see 'em as cold-blooded killers.'

Daley stood up and finishing off the coffee, picked up the telegraph forms and made his way to the gaol-house. Passing the hotel adjoining the Lone Puncher saloon he saw Red Carlson entering the hotel, and pondered briefly on what could have got Red up so early as he entered the gaol-house.

Clint and Mex were spruce and clean after the tub Lew Mallin had prepared for them, and were just enjoying a mug of coffee apiece when Daley came into the cell block. They made no comment when he unlocked the cell, throwing the gate open. He tossed the telegrams on the bunk and sat down heavily on the other bunk.

'I guess they're good enough for me,' Daley said as Clint read the telegrams and passed them on to Mex. 'I'm taking it that Father Dewar's got plumb bad eyesight.'

'Nope. I guess his eyesight's as good as yours, Sheriff,' Clint said quietly. 'My opinion is we were crowding him some and he wanted us out of the way.'

Daley's eyebrows lifted but he did not press for an explanation.

'What about young Sullivan?' asked Mex, nodding towards the next cell. 'You letting him out as well?'

Sheriff Daley's face hardened as he shook his head. 'Now that's something plumb different. All I had against you was say-so, but I saw that young killer with my own eyes. No sir, I reckon on my testimony he'll swing.'

'You've got to do your job the way you see it, Sheriff, but I'll stake everything I've got on Matt Sullivan being innocent,' Mex put in gently. 'He says he didn't kill Reardon an' I take his word for it.'

'That goes double,' Clint said flatly. 'So just don't rush the fences, Sheriff, and hurry that necktie party or we'll have to take sides.'

'You taking sides isn't going to alter the law taking its course in Portales, Bellamy,' said the sheriff, the friendliness dropping from his face. 'It's run straight without fear or favour.'

'I'm not saying it isn't and I'm not blaming you for jumping to the conclusion young Sullivan's a killer. You saw him with his hands on the knife and in the circumstances any man would need a lot of convincing he didn't do the killing. It's just that we believe him.'

'You bring me the proof and he goes free, but I can't hold back the attorney for long on a murder trial. Portales is a clean town and we always dole out justice fast.'

There was nothing more to be said and the pards looked in on Matt Sullivan before

131

collecting their gear. Matt lay on his bunk, the picture of misery. The depth of Kathy's depravation as he thought, appalled him and he had nothing to hold on to.

Red Carlson, the owner of the Lone Puncher Hotel was a lecherous man. A strong, heavy-shouldered, six-footer in his mid-thirties. Strikingly handsome and careful of his appearance. Women vied with each other for his attention and he took what he wanted wherever and whenever he chose. When the Irish immigrant entered Portales he had been at the door and it was then he realized what a frowsy lot of women he was wasting his virility upon. Even with the trail dust lying thick upon her face and clothing, the beauty of Kathy Mullins showed through, and Red Carlson had been immediately consumed with a desire to possess the girl.

The memory of her lingered, souring him against his own dance hostesses, and as the news of Portales filtered through to him he felt that things were working out his way. Three of her companions were in gaol, one was dead and one had left town. That put her to his reckoning out on a limb.

Normally Carlson slept until an hour or so short of midday. Night life was what he liked and what made his pile, so he felt no loss in missing a few hours of daylight. This morning however, he was up bright and early, and after breakfasting took a few breaths of air on the sidewalk before re-entering the hotel. Mojave Lord, the old receptionist-cum-handyman, was nodding sleepily in his cubby hole and Carlson ignored him. He pulled the register towards him and glanced at the last page. He climbed the stairs with a complete absence of noise and at Kathy Mullins' door paused and listened.

A delighted smile lit his face when he heard the sounds of sluicing and quietly tried the door. It was locked but he slipped his own key into the hole. Noiselessly turning the key pushed the door open a little.

Kathy Mullins was stripped to the waist washing her face and neck. Red Carlson stood stock still, drinking in the lissom beauty of the girl. Her raven-black hair gleamed where the shaft of sunlight touched it through the window, but Carlson's eyes were drawn to the milk-white young breasts that stood out round and firm. He thrust the door open and stepped into the room, closing the door behind him.

Kathy Mullins turned around with a gasp of dismay. For a long time she stood facing Carlson, mesmerized with mortification, her hands at her side. The man came in, a high flush of excitement on his face, and he had to hold himself in to stop rushing his fences.

Kathy backed away, searching behind her

for the towel which she had placed on a chair. She found it, wrapped it around herself as Carlson sat down on the edge of her bed. He grinned at the mounting rage on her face and her embarrassment as the towel slipped, revealing one smooth breast.

'No need to worry, ma'am. You ain't got nothing to hide I haven't seen before,' he said smoothly.

'What do you want?' she gasped.

Carlson waved a hand airily. 'Want to do you some good, ma'am. The way I see it, you're in a tough spot, all on your lonesome in a town like Portales, I guess somebody's gotta look out for you.' He looked away, giving her time to adjust the towel.

Kathy's first impulse was to tell him where to take his offer of help, but her embarrassment and rage melted away quite quickly. It was not the first time she had been surprised when washing by a long way. Throughout the trip from her Irish home men and women had been thrown so close together that one had to strike a bargain between cleanliness and propriety. There was a lot to think about in Carlson's words and she took time answering. Her position was difficult. She was alone, with no money, at least not enough money to last out more than a couple of weeks.

Carlson's face was turned away from her in profile and as she searched for words she could not help but notice his finely chiselled features.

'And why would you want to help me?' she asked at length.

'I'll tell you why, ma'am. I took a shine to you as soon as I saw you yesterday. I guess you look like no other women I ever knew and I'd like to know you better.' Kathy did not reply, so he continued, 'My moniker's Carlson, Redvers Carlson, I own this hotel, the saloon and a hardware store opposite. I guess there's nothing my woman couldn't have that money could buy.'

'So you want to buy me?'

Carlson nodded, unabashed. 'That's the size of it,' he replied. 'Might as well make the proposition clear. You say yes and I'll get a form made out an' signed up legally to give you a third share in my holdings.'

Kathy gasped at the man's brash effrontery and struggled hard for words.

'No man takes me before he marries me,' she said at last. Her big blue eyes stared hard into Carlson's light grey ones until he had the grace to look away. His glance returned quickly however, and as he watched the light flush spread over her features he told himself he had never seen a woman to equal her.

'I don't set much store by marriage,' he drawled, standing up. 'One thing though, if you take my offer you don't so much as look at another man.'

For one brief moment Kathy felt like saying yes. Carlson offered a roof, security and easy living in exchange for what could turn out to be a pleasure. Did her future hold anything better? Without hardly knowing why she shook her head.

'As I said, Mister Carlson, whoever takes me marries me first.'

He nodded slowly as though wondering whether to offer marriage, then with a slow smile he turned towards the door. Kathy turned away to collect the clothes she had left upon a chair and failed to see his swift change of direction. She was leaning slightly forward when he came behind her. His hands reached around her, found her breasts and he pulled her back tight to him. She pummelled and squirmed but to no avail. Carlson held her tight.

The excitement was back in Carlson as he slewed the girl around just enough to reach her face and his lips found hers eagerly. Kathy's mind was a whirl. There was fire in the man's kiss and his hands fondled her in a practised manner. Her mind told her to resist but her whole body screamed out to give way. Instinctively she fought but she made no impression upon him and as the passion of his kiss clawed its way to her vitals, her struggles ceased. Sensing he had her when his mouth sought hers again her lips were parted and he felt a sudden surge of the passion he had tapped as her body came forward tight.

The mists cleared from Kathy's mind and the situation became startlingly clear to her as someone knocked at the door. She tore herself away from Carlson, her face working with anger, and grabbing her dress struggled into it at the same time shouting a muffled 'Come in!' Carlson swore and glared towards the doorway. His eyes became wary when he recognized the two men Luke Daley had taken into custody.

Clint and Mex took in the situation quickly enough.

'This jasper worrying you, Kathy?' Clint's voice was flat.

The tears were beginning to run as the girl nodded and Mex crossed over to her. Carlson looked on, watchful but completely happy in his ability to cope.

'I made her a proposition, mister,' Carlson said as he sized up the stocky Texan. 'Anything else that happened was her idea.'

'You, mister, are a plain, no-good liar.' Bellamy let the words drip from his lips like ice chips falling to the floor. The girl's sobs told him all he wanted to know. 'If you're as much a man as you've been trying to prove try going for that shooting iron of yours.'

Carlson's eyelids hooded a little as he studied the Texan more closely, and a niggling doubt crept into his mind. He cast a quick look at the Mexican who stood close to the girl and the bitter glare he received increased the doubt to near panic. He struggled to regain his poise and only partially succeeded.

The seconds dragged away as he summoned the will to draw whilst Clint Bellamy stood relaxed and contemptuous, giving him the first move. Carlson went for his gun in a blur then spun and cursed as the gun was shot clean out of his hand. Before he could recover Clint was in close to him and thudding heavy blows into his body.

Rough-housing was something Carlson thought he knew all about, and his face grimaced savagely as he backed a little to get the measure of his man, but the Texan bore in, caught him with a jolting right to the throat, a couple of hard lefts to the mouth and a pile-driving right to the solar plexus that seemed to go right through his body. Carlson folded with a gasp then straightened and staggered as Clint really went to work on him.

Clint punished Carlson unmercifully. Time and time again when the man would have fallen he straightened him with a right to the chin then at long last he let Carlson slide to the ground, his face a gory mess, and as Clint surveyed his bruised knuckles ruefully the door opened and Sheriff Daley strode in. He took in the scene quickly enough and guessed at the truth.

'There was shooting,' he barked, staring at Clint who glowered back at him.

'Yeah! That's so. And I'm not so sure I did right. I should have put that slug right through this *hombre's* hide.'

Daley digested this and turned to Kathy Mullins who had regained some of her composure. 'You got any charges against Carlson?' he asked.

The girl looked quickly at the man's bruised and battered face then back to the sheriff. She shook her head slowly.

'No. Just get him out of here.'

Daley scratched his head as he regarded Carlson's recumbent form. 'That's kinda hard, lady, seeing that this place belongs to him. It'll maybe help if I keep him in the gaol-house for the rest of the day.' Daley turned to the few onlookers who had followed him up the stairs after the shot. 'Give a hand an' get Carlson to the hoosegow.'

Three men swarmed in and between them they lifted Carlson's unconscious form and hurried away with him. Daley watched them go then turned to the girl with an apologetic look on his face.

'I'm sorry Carlson bothered you, ma'am,' he said before leaving. 'If he causes you any more trouble I'll run him out of the territory.'

There was an embarrassed silence in the room for a minute as Kathy wanted to thank the pardners for arriving so opportunely yet did not want to enlarge upon the fate that had been spared her. The pards, sensing her embarrassment were equally tongue-tied, then Mex broke the silence.

'You take time out to get ready, Miss Kathy, and we'll wait down below for you. We can talk while you eat.'

Kathy smiled and nodded. Tears still glistened in her eyes but she was in control of herself now. When the pards left the room she locked the door in order to put on items of clothing she had omitted, then she hurried downstairs to meet Bellamy and Juarez who were talking to the oldster at the reception desk. They took the girl to the restaurant and drank coffee while they waited for her breakfast to be cooked. The coffee relaxed her and they reckoned now was the time to talk.

'Y'know, Kathy,' Clint said, 'Matt says he didn't kill Reardon.'

The girl's eyes widened as she stared from one to the other. 'Oh, if only it were true, but it can't be. I saw Jamie Reardon only a couple of minutes earlier. He – he tried–' She tailed off and the pards knew what he had tried and guessed why Matt had rushed away from her saying he would kill Reardon. They glanced significantly at each other. Even if Matt had done the killing, Kathy had only to give this evidence and he would get away with his life.

'I'd like to think Matt was man enough to admit to anything he'd done,' Mex said, his handsome face serious. 'So I'm taking the view he didn't do the killing.'

Kathy shook her head in distress. The time factor between seeing Reardon alive and dead, the white heat of Matt's rage as he left her pointed so surely to him being the killer she was unable to grasp any alternative.

'Kelly left town last night with the cross,' Clint remarked. 'He didn't do the killing. The sheriff can vouch for that, but he might know something.'

Both Kelly and the cross Kathy dismissed with an impatient shrug.

'We've got to make our decision,' Clint was continuing. 'Either we let Matt take his chance in a trial with you saying what made him go looking for Reardon, or we take him out of that gaol and find who should be in his place. Either way gives us time. On your evidence he'll get no more than a stretch in gaol.'

The thought of saying what she had to say in open court made Kathy shrink.

'What would happen to him if I didn't give evidence?' she asked.

'They'll hang him,' Mex said bluntly. 'Right or wrong they'll hang him.'

Kathy's lips trembled. 'I couldn't let them do that, but I never want to talk to him again if he did kill Reardon.'

'That's your affair,' Clint grunted then paused as the waiter placed an appetizing breakfast in front of the girl. 'But you'll ride with us if we spring him out of the gaol?' he asked when the waiter had left.

Kathy wondered why the pards were prepared to go to such lengths to save Matt. Not for one moment did she realize they would have done most anything on her account even if they had doubts concerning Matt. Her mind ran on as she ate. The law might overtake them at some other place and all three men would be imprisoned. That would leave her to fend for herself again and the same fate would probably await her from rougher hands than Carlson's, and without the same guarantee of security.

'I'll ride with you,' she said, looking up from her plate briefly, and the pards grinned back at her encouragingly.

Later they collected their gear and made their way to the livery stable. With some reluctance they struck a bargain with the livery man for the horses they had hoped to take with them to the wagon train, and contented themselves with four saddle-horses and a pack-horse.

They bought and stowed provisions on the pack-horse then Mex and the girl headed south out of town with the pack-horse tethered to the Mexican's saddle cantle. Clint crossed the street and tethered his dun gelding and a well muscled coal-black mustang to the hitchrail not far from the gaol. A number of folk eyed him curiously, but he ignored them and entered the gaol.

Lew Mallin and Luke Daley were looking through a few dodgers that had just arrived on the stage from Elida. Clint nodded casually when Daley looked up and eyed him frostily.

'Well, Bellamy, what can we do for you?'

Clint came straight to the point. 'You can let young Sullivan loose until we find the killer.'

The two lawmen stiffened.

'Don't be a goldarned fool, Bellamy,' the sheriff growled. 'You know I can't do that. We've been over what I saw before so there's no point in saying it again.'

'Can't blame you I guess, so that leaves me just one thing to do,' the Texan said slowly.

'Like what!?' The question came from Lew Mallin who had eased away from the table.

Clint shrugged his wide shoulders. 'I'll just have to take him.'

A tight grin stole over Mallin's features.

'You're sure bucking the odds if you're set on doing just that, mister,' he said evenly. 'Howcome you think we've kept the law in this territory?'

'You're good lawmen right enough,' Clint replied. 'It's just that this is one case that's not so cut and dried as it looks. If you turn

143

through your list of dodgers far enough back you'll find a *hombre* named Belman. We figure that Father Dewar is Belman, and either Belman or Kelly are headed south now carrying a king's ransom in gold and diamonds that Reardon had when he was killed.'

Daley opened up a drawer without a word and riffed through a pile of faded papers. The last but one he tossed on to the table. Mallin leaned forward to stare at it. It was not a good photograph but both lawmen agreed there were similarities between Belman and Father Dewar.

Clint went on to tell them the story of the cross and what had happened to the wagon train. He also told them why Matt had threatened to kill Reardon and when he had finished they were more than halfway to being convinced.

'If young Sullivan turns out to be guilty I'll return him to you in Portales,' Clint went on. 'But if we catch up with the killer you'll get full details.'

Daley's face was troubled as he looked at the earnest Texan.

'Y'know, Bellamy, I'd like to go along with you but it's not that easy. I've got to answer to other people.'

He stood up and crossed to the door to the cells which stood wide open and slammed it shut. When he returned he was looking into Clint's gun muzzle and Mallin was stood very still, almost disbelieving the speed of the Texan's draw.

'You've had the all-clear on Juarez and myself from a couple of good lawmen, sheriff, so you should believe we wouldn't buck the law unless we were sure of things. I'm taking Sullivan and I'm locking you in a cell just to ease your own problems, but if you want, we'll wait for Mallin just outside town if you'll let him ride along with us.' Clint's eyes shifted a little to Mallin. 'I guess you can be trusted not to rustle up a posse.'

Daley ignored the gun and glanced at his deputy who nodded.

'It sounds fair enough, Luke,' said Mallin and the sheriff shrugged resignedly.

Clint crossed to the wall and unhooking a big ring holding a couple of keys, tossed it to Mallin.

'Take one off then you can let yourselves out after I've cleared.'

The deputy did so then the two lawman unhitched their gunbelts and laid them on the table. They led the way into the cell block and Carlson's bitter eyes watched Clint as he hustled the lawmen into a cell. Clint ignored him and unlocked Matt Sullivan's cell. The Irishmen looked on uncomprehendingly and Clint had to haul him on to his feet and push him out of the cell before the youngster realized he was being freed.

Carlson had heard the earlier conversation

about the cross with its rings of precious stones and the thought was already with him that he might combine the acquisition of the cross with his intention to wreak vengeance on Bellamy. He watched as they hurried out of the cell block and he determined to get sworn in on a posse and get his chance under the cloak of legality.

CHAPTER TEN

Daylight chased the terrors away for Kelly and he felt the mad surge of elation course through him as he struggled straight in the saddle against the weight of the cross. His eyes widened in sheer joy and he laughed loud and long. The wonder of his good fortune kept running through his mind; no more struggling, just ease and lush living. A momentary spasm of unease crossed his mind at the problem of realizing on the cross, but he thrust the thought away. Kelly's elation was short-lived. As the sun climbed clear the haze closed in, and the Irishman found himself expecting at any moment for riders to burst through in pursuit of him. The weight of the cross irritated him and he realized that carrying it in one piece constituted his greatest danger. With it cut into lengths and in his saddle-bags he could enter any town without exciting comment.

His first impulse was to dismount and set to work but he realized he would have to find cover. Any rider coming upon him busy at that chore would kill without compunction, so he heaved the cross into a more comfortable position and kept his sights on

147

the hills, now clear of the haze. He stopped at a stream to slake his parched throat and to allow his horse to drink its fill, then consumed with impatience he waited for the animal to take a much-needed meal from the lush tall grass growing at the water's edge. He spent the time squinting into the distance until finally climbing back into the saddle, drummed his heels into the unfortunate animal's ribs to head for the canyon now just a short distance ahead.

Around the first bend of the canyon, Kelly saw a narrow offshoot and scrambling down to the ground, he checked upon its possibilities for the job in hand. It opened out after twenty yards into a big, blank-ended cavern. Returning to the canyon he led his horse into the cavern and struggled out of the harness, letting the cross fall to the floor. A couple of minutes passed as he rubbed the pain out of his back and shoulders then falling to his knees, he tore feverishly at the fastening studs. With his eyes shining in anticipation he pulled the flaps aside and went to grasp the cross. His hands stayed in mid-air and his eyes dilated as he stared down.

The sobs started from deep down. Long inhuman sobs that turned to wailing, crying and cursing, then Kelly was beating the floor of the cavern with his fists, unmindful of the pain as the skin broke on his knuckles and the blood flowed. He stood up and ran around the cavern, thumping the walls and shrieking oaths. He pounded the horse, sending the animal into a slithering run down the passage into the canyon and away to freedom. Kelly did not even notice the horse was gone. The shock deranged him completely and he alternated between crazy laughter and crying until at long last he fell down from sheer exhaustion and fell asleep sprawled over the fake cross.

Belman saw Kelly's mount when he passed the mouth of the canyon to skirt the hills. The animal was browsing from the long grass near the stream, so he moved with care in case the rider was laying for him, but common sense told him that no man set in ambush would leave his horse in full view. Realizing the animal was alone, Belman pushed on around the squat hills, taking the long way to his next objective, Elida.

Mex and Kathy Mullins edged their mounts forward from behind the huddle of junipers towards the trail when they recognized Clint and Matt Sullivan riding out from Portales. The third rider was Lew Mallin. Mex smiled to himself. It looked like Clint had struck a bargain.

There were brief nods when the riders met but Kathy Mullins and Matt Sullivan sat their mounts like carved images, both avoiding the other. When Mex led the way Kathy edged her horse alongside his pinto. Matt rode behind, with Mallin and Clint.

Mex tried conversation to thaw the girl out but she was too conscious of Matt and too certain of his guilt to indulge in light talk, so at last the Mexican gave it up. Matt studied the slim form ahead of him with an intensity almost akin to hate. What a fool he had been to be taken in by her! Any woman who could stand by and see her lover gaoled for her crime was beneath his contempt.

When they stopped for a meal under the shelter of an overhang, the boy and girl sat as far away from each other as possible and each took the stony-faced silence of the other as a manifestation of guilt. Their companions tried ignoring the situation but they wondered at the Irishman's attitude. They could understand the girl's belief in Matt's guilt under the circumstances of Reardon's death but they failed to understand why Matt should be so stiff-necked. It was when they were remounting that the answer came to Clint. With a muttered excuse to Lew Mallin he pushed his gelding to the front alongside Mex and Kathy Mullins. His pard squinted across at him questioningly.

'Y'know, Kathy,' Clint began. 'Circumstantial evidence of guilt isn't enough to condemn anyone.'

Kathy Mullins gave him a quick surprised

glance. 'It depends how strong the circumstances are, Mister Bellamy,' she replied quietly.

Clint shook his head. 'I reckon it'll surprise you to know that two people out of this little party are thought to be killers, both suspected of the same killing. It seems to you impossible that anyone but Matt could have killed Reardon. Well, I'm betting my last dime that he thinks you killed Reardon.'

'Me!' Kathy was startled. 'How could I...?' She tailed off.

'Just think back. He finds you distressed and you tell him you've just had some trouble with Reardon and straight away he finds Reardon with a knife in him.'

'But a few minutes had passed before I told Matt about Reardon,' the girl protested.

'Yeah. That same few minutes makes all the difference between innocence and guilt. By my reckoning that young feller's thinking some mighty bad things about you for letting him take the blame.'

The colour flooded the girl's face briefly then she became deathly pale and as the Mexican's sharp eyes picked up a lead that took them off the trail and across country, she held her mount back until Matt came alongside her. Clint wheeled his gelding around and waited for Lew Mallin.

For a few moments the two youngsters rode together in an awkward silence, Matt looking straight ahead trying to ignore the girl's sorrowful expression. When Kathy leaned towards him and touched his arm, the slight pressure sent a thrill of excitement through him despite his thoughts, and he swivelled his head involuntarily to look at her. The moisture glistening in her expressive eyes weakened his resolve.

'I – I'm sorry, Matt,' she said quietly.

Sullivan took her simple statement to imply that she was sorry she had let him take the blame.

'Well! What are you going to do about it? Are you going to tell that lawman what happened?'

This confirmation of Bellamy's surmise started the tears rolling down her cheeks but she pulled herself together and shook her head. Matt's face grew hard again.

'Matt! You've been all wrong! I didn't kill Reardon!' There was a couple of minutes silence. 'And I've been wrong too,' she continued. 'I thought you must have done it.'

Matt Sullivan's face unfroze and the light sprang back into his eyes. His hand reached out to hers and all their troubles melted in the happiness the contact sent coursing through them. Clint Bellamy smiled with quiet satisfaction as he took time off from talking to Lew Mallin to watch them.

'Tell me, why has Juarez headed off the trail?' the deputy broke in on Clint's absorption. 'That Kelly's tracks ran straight on and he's the *hombre* who's toting the cross you told me about.'

Clint nodded. 'Yeah, that's so. Kelly's got the cross, but we reckon Belman's the one to trail. If Kelly's got the cross then it's our opinion Belman's sure got plans for him.'

The deputy shrugged his shoulders. He was committed to following the lead of the pards, and after being in their company for just this short time he had formed the opinion he could do a lot worse.

They rested briefly where Belman had stopped for a couple of hours. He had removed traces of the fire where he had cooked his breakfast but Mex, in a diligent search, found some scattered ashes. Mallin approved the Mexican's thoroughness. He reflected, it is only by knowing everything about your quarry that you can gauge his state of mind and arrive at the best time to take him. He concluded that Belman gave all the signs of being a hard man to corner. The sort of man who conserved his strength and that of his horse.

Some way behind them a man with all of Belman's qualifications rode in company with three hard-looking companions. Red Carlson was intent on gaining possession of the cross Bellamy had spoken of in addition to settling his account with the Texan. Daley had released him without much preamble after Mallin had departed in pursuit of Bellamy, and Carlson had wasted no time before gathering together his own particular henchmen and riding south. In Portales he had interests that brought a steady stream of money into his account, but like all men of his breed the thought of unlimited wealth at one swoop was too much to resist.

He had read the sign quite easily and knew that Bellamy and Sullivan had waited for Lew Mallin and had then joined two others whom he deduced to be the girl and Mex Juarez with a led horse, and so, he reasoned, all but the girl would have to die. Thoughts of possessing Kathy Mullins set him aflame with desire, and in the circumstances killing her companions would be an added pleasure.

When Mex led his party off the trail Carlson had them in view and throughout the day he and his men kept in touch with the group ahead, a feat that was not so remarkable considering that Carlson had obtained the capital to start his Portales ventures through numerous rustling forays down in Arizona and had cleared the territory without once coming under the eagle eye of the law.

Mex Juarez eased his pinto to a stop just below the ridge of a long-humped hill and waited for the others to catch up. He pointed to where a narrow stream lost itself behind the furthest of two big hills. The mere dot that emerged now and again out of the haze they took to be a horse and Mex, whose eyesight was as keen as an eagle's, confirmed the impression.

'That's a cayuse,' he said quietly. 'Been there a long time too. Had its fill of feed and water so I guess something's happened to the rider.' He pointed to the trail he was following. 'Belman went that way but I doubt whether that's his cayuse.'

Clint and Mallin nodded their agreement. Kathy and Matt were too absorbed in each other to waste time on speculation and when the others moved over the ridge they urged their mounts on mechanically. They came to earth a little shame-facedly when Clint dropped back and issued a stern warning.

'You two keep your eyes skinned and ride where you're told to ride. There's mebbe a killer holed up in those hills all primed to take us one by one if we show ourselves.'

'Sure thing, Mister Bellamy,' Matt replied. 'We'll do just like you say.'

Clint smiled reassuringly and moved on ahead. 'Keep right tight behind me and keep low in the saddle.'

They did as they were told and the party arrived at a point close to where the horse stood nodding in sleep. The trail was just below them and a short distance away it entered the canyon that split the two hills. As they studied the hills the mystery of the lone cayuse was cleared. A large figure came staggering out of the canyon, carrying what was unquestionably the cross.

'Kelly!'

The name rolled off the tongues of Matt and Kathy and Clint recognized the Irishman immediately. They glanced at each other in some surprise. For Kelly to be alive, in one piece, and still in possession of the cross was cause for surprise.

The Irishman might have been in one piece but it was evident that something was radically wrong with him. Staggering from side to side he flung his arms about like a man demented and at last they heard the screaming, babbling talk that bubbled from his lips.

'He's sure enough crazy,' Mallin growled. 'Let's get to him.' He eased his horse out of cover and started down to the trail. The others followed him and they stopped abreast on the trail just about fifty yards away from the approaching Irishman.

Kelly was not registering anything and he gave no sign of having seen the phalanx of riders ahead of him. His screaming torrent of words were completely unintelligible. Lew Mallin eased ahead of the others. Kelly stopped, suddenly aware of the group across the trail and the lawman bearing down upon him, and bubbles of froth foamed out of the corners of his mouth.

'It's mine! It's mine!' he screamed, and went in a lurching run towards the canyon mouth. As Mallin increased his mount's speed to overtake the Irishman, Clint and Mex saw what had unbalanced the man. The flaps of the canvas cover were wide open and enough of the cross was showing to convince the pards that Kelly carried nothing but lumber. As Mallin caught up with Kelly and tried to calm him, Clint turned to the youngsters:

'You say the cross you brought from Ireland is made of pure gold?'

'Yes, Mister Bellamy. Solid gold through and through,' Matt answered.

'Then that one Kelly's carrying is sure enough a fake,' Mex put in dryly. 'Seems like finding out sent him plumb loco.'

They were about to go to Mallin's assistance as Kelly lunged furiously at the lawman but Mallin's patience was thin and the next time he eased his mount within range of the demented Irishman he brought his gun butt down on the man's head, sending him sprawling into the dust. Mallin looked at the cross as the pards stopped their mounts beside the luckless Kelly.

'So that's the cross that's worth a fortune,' he growled. His eyes had lost some of their friendliness and his expression grew soured.

Matt and Kathy were staring at the cross in utter disbelief but Clint and Mex were unmoved.

They slid to the ground and Mex fastened the flaps of the canvas cover before turning Kelly over and making him more comfortable. Clint glanced at Matt.

'Collect his cayuse,' he said. 'I guess we'll have to take him along.'

Sullivan departed immediately and Lew Mallin stamped around impatiently while they waited for his return with the led horse. The lawman stopped every now and again to glare at Bellamy and Juarez who were smoking, both totally unmoved by events.

'It adds up,' Clint remarked. 'Belman must have worked the switch. If Kelly had been carrying the right cross he'd have been buzzard meat by now. I believe the switch was worked just around the time Reardon got his comeuppance.'

'Yeah, it's plain enough,' agreed Mex. 'Belman's crossed this trail while that cayuse grazed where we found it, and the fact he left Kelly severely alone makes it nigh certain his pack-horse is carrying the real thing.'

When Matt returned with Kelly's horse they draped the unconscious man over his saddle, leaving the fake cross in its harness on his back. As they climbed back into their saddles Lew Mallin eyed his companions with a look of lingering doubt.

'Maybe when this *hombre* comes to I'll get to know just what to believe.'

Mex shrugged away his remark and pushed his pinto out in front to pick up Belman's trail around the western side of the two humped hills.

Red Carlson lay at the rim of a fold in the ground, hidden by the thick tufts of bunch-grass that grew in profusion on the sloping land below the timber. A wide smile of satisfaction lit his handsome face as he saw clear evidence of the fortune he was chasing. He could make out the object carried by Kelly but the distance was too great for him to see what the open flaps revealed. The bit of by-play when Kelly turned and ran from the party he construed as the natural action of a man aiming to keep a fortune to himself, and when the party continued on afterwards away from Portales around the furthermost hill, he concluded the cross was of sufficient value to make Lew Mallin defect from his lawman job in favour of a share.

Carlson reckoned they would keep in close to the bottom of the hill and his mind played around a picture of the terrain between his present position and Elida. It took him a couple of seconds to decide that the west side of Cherokee Gap was the ideal spot to ambush the unsuspecting party ahead. The canyon in front of him ran a full ten miles with Cherokee Gap about seven miles distant. The gap itself split the west hill in almost a straight line.

'They've caught up with the *hombre* with the cross,' he remarked when his henchmen lined up beside him. 'And they're heading around the hills. We'll burn leather and lay for 'em the other side of Cherokee Gap.'

'That shows good sense, Red.' The speaker was Amos Greer, a dark, menacing figure astride a spirited palomino. His companions, Sam Morse and Gabe Wells nodded. 'We should get 'em cold.'

Red Carlson's bitter eyes swivelled around his henchmen as he prepared to swing into the saddle. 'Just take good care you don't put a bullet in the girl,' he growled. 'I've got my own plans for her.'

His crew grinned knowingly at each other. They preferred hard liquor and faro themselves but they were happy to allow him his preferences.

The four horsemen rode out of cover and down to the trail. They allowed their mounts to drink sparingly at the stream then travelled at speed through the canyon. When they turned into Cherokee Gap they just cleared the main canyon before the Elida-Portales Stage swept through, and Carlson permit-ted himself a tight smile of satisfaction as he listened to the clatter of shod hooves and the rumbling of the hard-driven coach.

'I guess we're in luck,' he said with a grin. 'Old Mayhew's pretty tight-lipped but the less anyone sees the better.'

As Carlson had said it was better that no-one saw them. Life in Portales was pleasurable enough for them to want to return to it.

They made a fast ride through Cherokee Gap even though the width only permitted single file. Gabe Wells bringing up the rear got the main benefit of the thick carpet of dust that had gathered throughout the months of disuse and all the time he rode blind with the billowing clouds stirred up by his companions swirling around his head. Always a bit short on temper he was in a sullen rage by the time they came out of the gap and headed uphill to the cover of the boulders that ranged like man-made fortresses. His companions took up their positions carelessly indifferent to the job ahead but Gabe Wells allowed his resentment to boil until he itched to get someone in his sights. He felt he could not spill blood soon enough.

'There they come.'

Red Carlson drawled the words and pointed to where the shoulders of the hill stood out beyond a long concave sweep. One after another riders emerged into view until six ridden horses and one pack-horse cleared the shoulder and moved inexorably into rifle range.

CHAPTER ELEVEN

Lew Mallin gave Clint and Mex questioning glances when they pulled their mounts up just a mile beyond the big bluff. Neither had a specific reason for stopping except for feelings that things were not what they seemed. They had ridden the lonely trails a long time and had developed a keen intuitive sense that had no logical basis, and at this moment this sixth sense was working overtime in both men.

'The trail's clear enough,' Mallin said at length. 'What's the matter?'

'Nothing maybe,' Clint answered briefly.

Mex turned in his saddle after scrutinizing the hill slope into the distance.

'Just a feeling we're hugging the hill too close,' he said, catching Clint's eye. 'We'll ride wide and maybe pick up the trail a few miles further on.'

'It's all right by me if you *hombres* are spooky,' Mallin grunted, then he nearly swallowed his words as metal winged past his head by the merest fraction.

The squeal of a horse came a split second before the report from Gabe Wells' rifle and the horse bearing Kelly whirled around, a

163

searing bullet burn across its withers, and shot off in a mad run the way they had come.

Wells' provident itchy finger galvanized the group into action. As they ducked low in the saddle and kneed their mounts into a run from the foot of the hill Mex leaned across to young Matt Sullivan.

'Get after Kelly and ride wide when you catch him.'

Matt waved his hand in answer, his eyes ablaze with excitement as he turned his horse in a wide arc, and crouching low, went away fast in the wake of Kelly's maddened mount. Kathy Mullins gave him a wild-eyed look as he went past, then without thinking, she broke away from Clint's side and followed.

Gabe Wells' impatience to taste blood saved the day for them. Even with their intention of travelling wide they might still have come much closer to the guns of Carlson and his men, but now they knew the score and played the game out their way.

Well beyond the range of the riflemen they drew to a halt and considered the next move. The guns had stopped firing, but they reckoned the ambushers were still under cover awaiting developments. Clint squinted backtrail where the unconscious Kelly was being borne at speed ahead of Matt and Kathy. He reckoned they would come to no harm so long as he and the other two men contained the would-be killers in their present spot.

'I guess we'd better get around the back of these *hombres,* Mex,' he said, and his pard's black eyes glittered wickedly when he nodded. 'If you'll stay right here, Mallin, and signal any movement by those *hombres* to us we'll take 'em from both sides.' Mallin grunted his assent.

They split company, Clint turning his mount north and Mex heading south whilst Mallin sat back in the saddle and rolled himself a smoke. The passivity of his role irked him, but the lawman had the good sense to appreciate the value of his job should the men on the hill break from cover. He failed to see Carlson make his move because of the deep fold that lay beyond the jutting eroded rocks from whence the rifle fire had come, and Clint was too late to see Carlson make his way under cover along the face of the hillside.

'You blamed fool!' Carlson yelled at Gabe Wells. 'What in hades made you let loose at this range?' His glance of pure venom was enough to make the case-hardened Wells shudder but the expression changed as he squinted again towards their intended victims. An evil grin spread over his face as he leaned over and slapped Wells' shoulder. 'Nope! I guess you did just right.'

His companions, returning their attention

to the scene saw what gave Carlson so much pleasure. The cross and the girl were heading in one direction whilst the lawman, Bellamy and Juarez were hazing out of range.

'They'll try coming in for you,' Carlson said quickly. 'Keep 'em busy for a couple of hours then you can fade away through the gap.'

'Which way do we head?' Amos Greer asked as Carlson got up.

'Portales. Where else?' returned Carlson. 'And set about fixing an alibi in case you don't give Mallin his comeuppance.'

The fold in the ground behind the ridged, natural fortresses of stone ran for a mile or so both sides of the gap, and just short of the mouth of the gap a rain channel ran down to floor level, giving adequate cover from watchers on the plains beyond, so all the advantages were with Carlson and his men.

Briefly Carlson emerged from cover as he rounded the shoulder of the hill, but stray shots from Greer and the others were claiming Mallin's attention at that moment, and Clint was already climbing the hill facing in the wrong direction.

Once out in the open with the three riders strung out a long way ahead of him, Carlson pushed his mount to top speed and in a surprisingly short time he was within rifle range. He levelled his rifle at the head of Kelly's horse then thought better of it. If only he could be sure that Greer and the others would finish off Mallin and the two pardners then he could have killed off the two men ahead and made off with the girl at his leisure, but he just could not take the chance.

As he considered, he eased his speed and at that moment Matt Sullivan caught up with Kelly's mount and hauled on its rein until it came to a fretful stop. Matt and the girl turned their mounts to face the side-gun Carlson had drawn in favour of the rifle. Kathy gasped in dismay, and Matt fought down the impulse to go for the little Derringer Mex Juarez had given him, which rested inside his shirt.

'So we meet again.' There was mockery in Carlson's eyes as he watched the hot flush mount her neck and cheeks. 'We'll start again from where we left off as soon as we get a bit of time,' he remarked casually. 'She sure is hot-blooded,' he continued, returning Matt's questioning look with a sneering smile.

'Oh Matt, Matt, don't listen to him,' Kathy cried. 'He tried to force me – but Clint and Mex stopped him.'

An evil laugh escaped from Carlson's lips then he became briskly businesslike.

'From now on just do exactly what I say. One false move, Sullivan, an' I'll put a slug in the young lady's belly.' The look accompanying the words convinced Matt that

Carlson would find fiendish pleasure in doing just what he said. 'Now, take that cross off that *hombre* an' shuffle yourself into the harness.'

'Do like he says, Matt,' Kathy said quickly, fearful for her man's life.

Matt nodded dully and slid to the ground. Kelly was beginning to grunt with returning consciousness but the youngster was able to slip the harness from under his armpits. As Matt put on the harness, Carlson's eyes glittered with anticipation as he considered the size of the cross, but he kept his patience in check. Time enough to gloat over it.

Carlson motioned Matt on to his horse then rode alongside Kelly. Still covering the two youngsters with his revolver he withdrew a long knife from its scabbard and sliced through the ropes that held the stirring man. Then with a sharp savage thrust he sunk the knife deep in Kelly's back. The Irishman recovered consciousness and died all within the space of a second. There was a gasp of horror from Kathy and a short period of retching as Carlson allowed the man to slither to the ground, then sent the horse running with a kick to the ribs.

Carlson turned his full attention to the other two and levelled his gun meaningly at the girl. 'Now get going! We want to make plenty of speed for the next hour or so, then maybe me and the girl can relax the way we like best.'

The eyes of both Matt and Kathy were riveted upon the grotesque corpse, but when Matt's gaze finally found Carlson, there was a quality in the level look that told Carlson the lad had just grown into a man. He determined to salivate the Irishman as soon as it suited his purpose.

Carlson forced the pace and headed around the northern end of the hill, then back south along the foot of the easternmost hill. The sun dropped from view when they arrived where the twin hills flattened out and merged with the undulating grassland. Large bunches of cattle were dotted here and there as far as Elida Peak, the towering mountain through which Silver Canyon ran straight to the long slope above Elida. Carlson swung east to avoid the main herds, all the time he kept up a bantering stream of conversation intended to reduce the girl's resistance and to stir up Matt's temper to breaking point.

Matt did not rise to the bait. He rode on stolidly, letting Carlson talk all he wanted. The little Derringer bounced around above Matt's waistband, giving him comfort and supreme confidence. Normally he could never contemplate killing a man in cold blood but remembering the vicious pleasure on Carlson's face when he had plunged the knife into Kelly time and again, he decided

169

that he would kill Carlson with similar despatch.

They made Elida Peak as the light faded, but once again Carlson decided against the direct run through the canyon and edged around the western side of the tall, snow-capped mountain. He called a halt beside a trickle of water that spilled out of the rock face and removed his rifle from the saddle boot as he dropped to the ground, then he prodded the barrel into Matt's back after the youngster had wriggled out of the cross harness.

'Jump to it, *hombre*. Get these cayuses watered and ground hitch 'em. Me and the girl have got things to do and mebbe later we'll eat.'

As Carlson spoke the thin light was sufficient for Matt to see the abject terror in Kathy's eyes. The thin circle of steel pressed tight into the small of his back, and in a flash of inspiration Matt realized that his best chance was now.

As he swivelled towards Kathy he felt the bullet singe its way through his clothing as Carlson pressed the trigger and as he continued his turn he gulped his relief at turning the right way. His fist met Carlson's jaw with a crunching blow that stopped the man in his tracks, making him drop his rifle.

Keeping up the advantage Matt stepped close and pumped a stream of punches at the man's face, all the savagery fermented by Carlson's taunts lending strength to the blows. Carlson had weathered a lot of rough-housing in his time however, and the mists cleared from his mind after Matt's first paralysing blow and a lot of the younger man's punches missed their target as he took evasive action. He moved in to trade punches and Matt gasped time after time as Carlson planted solid blows through his guard. The younger man's lack of experience was telling and Kathy watching in an agony of mind could see that the tide of Matt's luck was changing. The rifle was still on the ground near to the contestants' feet and she dashed forward to pick it up.

Carlson saw her intention and as she was about to reach for the rifle he gave her a smashing back-handed blow that sent her down in a heap. Tears of rage flooded Matt's eyes as he saw the girl's face covered in blood and he went in close, flailing punches wildly. Carlson slipped them easily and slammed a thudding right to the chin that sent Matt to the ground like a log. Matt's eyes closed briefly as Carlson stood over him, then the man turned his back contemptuously and moving to where the cross lay, knelt beside it to open the cover. With firm resolve Matt grasped the butt of the Derringer inside his shirt.

There was a long-drawn hiss as Carlson

eyed the fake cross, then he rose slowly, easing out his gun. He was a split second too late seeing the Derringer, and his last breath went in a curse of rage as the little gun spat flame.

Matt watched in a sort of dazed exultation as Carlson's gun dropped from nerveless fingers. Even in the thin moonlight he saw the spread of blood on the man's shirt, as Carlson staggered and pitched to the ground. A full minute passed before Matt was able to pull himself together, then he crossed to Carlson's still form and turned him over. He moved over to Kathy as she came back to consciousness and stared up at him out of large luminous eyes. He knelt beside her, cradling her head in his arms. Carlson's blow had split her lips and caused her nose to bleed but Matt did not think there was any permanent damage.

'I'll get some water and clean you up,' he said as he went to lower her gently but she sat up and stared around as memory flooded back. Her eyes fastened on Carlson's still form and she flashed a questioning glance at Matt.

'He's dead.' Matt spoke simply without any vestige of pride. 'He was drawing his guns to kill me when I shot him.'

'Thank God! Thank God!' There was a depth of feeling in the girl's voice. 'He was evil through and through.'

Matt pulled her close and they stayed locked in each other's arms for a long time, then later, after bathing her face, he hauled Carlson's body over his saddle, tying the corpse securely before remounting their horses and making their way back with Carlson's horse tethered to Matt's.

Clint Bellamy kept his mount moving uphill and all the time keeping some object of cover between him and the men further along the hill. When he judged himself to be out of rifle range he stopped the uphill climb and turned to the south. Briefly he emerged from cover and the guns opened fire from below, but they presented no danger. There was purpose in showing himself in the open. He wanted to draw their fire while Mex got in close.

Slipping his rifle out of his saddle holster, Clint dismounted and made his way downhill until he was almost within range, then sent a few tentative shots in the general direction. Staccato reports rolled up to him as a few more bullets travelled aimlessly up the hill, then the firing stopped.

The sun's rays, slanted by the peaks of the distant mountains bothered Clint as he squinted downhill. He failed to see Gabe Wells slip out of cover, to slither down the face of one rock to the shelter of another. In the half-hour that followed the guns were silent, with Clint waiting patiently for Mex to open up from close quarters, and Gabe Wells moving inexorably up and up.

It was evident to Clint that Mex was taking these men seriously. In fact so much time had elapsed that he reckoned his pard's caution was exaggerated, and he was just about to send a few bullets to spatter amongst the towering rocks below, when a puff of smoke whipped out of a huddle of boulders just a short distance from where the ambushers had taken cover. He heard the whine of the bullet as it soared past after ricocheting from a long, low slab of rock no more than fifty feet away from him.

Juarez's warning shot galvanized him into action and he threw himself sideways just a second before a bullet buried itself in the dust where he had lain. The gunfire started up in earnest down below but the man who had so patiently dogged Clint was nursing his bullets, and the Texan was suddenly aware that he faced formidable opposition.

Neither man fired as the sun finally slid down behind the big mountains, but both were studying the ground that separated one from the other. In twenty minutes it was dark and the gun flashes showed bright below, but Wells and Clint slipped out of cover simultaneously.

The first dark after sunset was thick, impenetrable, and both men relied entirely upon an acutely attuned sense of hearing.

Clint drew himself along the few yards of flat ground without a whisper of noise to the rim of the little fold that rose up on the other side to the low flat boulder that had sheltered the other man. Unseen by Clint, Gabe Wells paused at the rim on his side of the fold and listened. Together they slithered downhill towards each other, each pausing to listen at the same time. It was uncanny how the action of one was suited to the other, and they arrived at the bottom of the slopes together, unaware of each other until the last revealing second.

The Texan felt the man's hot breath on his face and instinctively rolled to his right. The man's gasp of surprise was only a split second in front of the gunshot that Clint would have collected in his skull if he had rolled in the other direction, then they were at grips with each other. Clint brought his gun barrel down hard on the man's hand, sending the other's gun slithering through the grass, then as his opponent squirmed and smashed blows at him he clawed for the man's neck. His hands closed around a thick strongly-muscled throat that felt as durable as an oak tree and he knew then he had one heck of a fight on his hands.

Gabe Wells, once committed, went to work enthusiastically. Always the irascible trouble-shooter for Red Carlson, he loved a fight and his triumphs over the years had left a trail of dead men and broken bones. As he started his clawing, gouging tactics he emitted his battle growl with something near to enjoyment, but the pleasure slipped away as his all-action methods failed to relax the grip on his throat. Clint's strong grip was beginning to bother him and Wells turned his attention to breaking the stranglehold.

Clint's hands came away at last but before Wells could congratulate himself, the same hands exploded a few times on his face and chin. The precision and power of the blows sent a tremor of uncertainty running through his mind, and squirming from under the Texan's body he rolled away, scrabbling for his other gun. Clint leapt after him and landed hard on the man as the gun cleared leather. The Texan's hand closed over the man's wrist and turned the gun away.

Gabe Wells was done with fighting. He wanted more than anything to bring the battle to a close, and he put all his bull strength into the struggle to bring his gun to bear. Perspiration stood out in huge drops along the Texan's forehead as the gun turned back inexorably in his direction. Wells fired prematurely and a bullet ploughed through Clint's clothing, taking away the first layer of skin from his thigh.

The burn galvanized Clint into action. Bunching his muscles, he let go of the man, simultaneously springing away and grabbing for his gun. He landed awkwardly and fell sideways as Wells followed his body around with his gun hand. Even as he hit the ground Clint fired then rolled away waiting for the man's next shot. The seconds ticked away and with his eyes becoming more and more accustomed to the dark the Texan stared hard at the still form at the foot of the fold. There was no movement, and at length he slithered to his opponent's side. He wiped the sweat out of his eyes as he saw the man was dead, then standing up Clint emitted a low whistle.

A couple of minutes later the dun gelding made its way down the little fold and stood off patiently while Clint manhandled Gabe Wells' body over the saddle. After a brief search the Texan recovered the gun he had dropped in the early stages of the battle then he led the horse downhill.

As he approached the place where the rifleman had lain in wait, one more shot rang out further to the right, followed by the cry of the cougar, and throwing his head back, the Texan gave a life-like imitation of the big cat's cry in reply.

So, it was over. Mex had got close enough to bring the fight to an end. Thankfully Clint headed openly for the big rocks. When he joined the Mexican, his pard was busy tying a corpse down to the saddle pommel. He paused to light a cheroot and by the light of the match Clint saw the satisfied gleam in his pard's black eyes.

'One *hombre* got clear but mebbe Mallin got him,' Mex said as he helped transfer the dead man from Clint's horse. 'There was a shot anyways after he headed down the grade.'

'Let's go see,' Clint replied. 'It was lucky for me you had your eyes peeled, Mex,' he added. 'That *hombre* would have plugged me for sure if it hadn't been for that warning shot of yours.'

The Mexican did not reply at once. His teeth flashed in the dark and he punched his pard playfully. 'I guess we've gotta look out for each other all the time,' he joshed. 'The trails could get awful lonesome.'

He swung astride his pinto and headed down the grade. Clint followed with the two led horses tethered behind. Mex was right. They had travelled together so long now that life would lose a lot of its lustre if things changed. They reached the mouth of Cherokee Gap and stayed still as Mallin's voice barked an order.

'Freeze you *hombres!*'

'That you, Mallin?' Clint called and they heard the lawman grunt before replying.

'Had to be careful. I collected a slug from the last polecat that came down the grade. He got clean away through the gap.'

Mallin rode alongside the pards and

peered through the gloom at the corpses. 'Couple of Carlson's men. Gabe Wells and Sam Morse. I thought there was something familiar about the *hombre* that plugged me. It was Amos Greer.'

'Carlson's men, eh?' Clint mused. 'I guess he thought he had a grudge. He was mighty lucky he didn't get to Boot Hill.'

'How about you, Mallin?' Mex put in. 'You hurt much?'

'No more'n a hunk of flesh outa my thigh. I fixed it up before you came along.'

Mex nodded and started to lead the way out of the canyon mouth.

'Ain't you going to head after Greer?' Mallin asked.

'Nope. Just ride back to where you left the others,' Mex replied.

'What others?' Mallin sounded aggrieved. 'They didn't come back. I reckon Sullivan took the chance to ride to hell and gone.'

Clint and Mex increased their speed as the sudden urgency of the situation gripped them leaving Mallin, to grunt and grumble before following.

CHAPTER TWELVE

'So now what!? Maybe you'll still say Sullivan's no killer?'

Mallin's tone was harsh. Clint and Mex said nothing. Kelly's body, sprawling grotesquely amidst the clumps of bunch-grass, had started off an unpleasant chain of thought in both their minds.

'Maybe we didn't look close enough at that cross,' Mallin went on. 'Could be it was just the case we were admiring.' He grunted in disgust. 'I reckon that Sullivan's laughing his head off right now.'

'Well if that's so he hasn't got much laughing left to him,' Mex growled. 'Let's get these men buried some place then we can travel light.'

'Nope. Let's get this one fixed on the pack-horse. I guess we like the ends sewn up for all to see in Portales and one sure way to keep the records straight is to pass dead men on to the funeral parlour for decent burial.'

Clint and Mex slid to the ground and man-handled Kelly's corpse on to the pack-horse without question then resuming their places in the saddle, Mex forged ahead with Clint and Mallin riding side by side, then behind them the other three horses strung out, bearing their dismal loads. When they rounded the mountain and crossed the canyon's mouth, Mex had difficulty in picking up the trail, and while he back-tracked and circled Clint and Mallin smoked a cigarette apiece and opened a couple of cans. Mex returned eventually and slipping out of the saddle, took the can of beans Clint proffered with unsimulated interest.

'Well?' Mallin growled. 'Lost 'em?'

There was a sudden flash of hostility in the Mexican's eyes as he glanced at Mallin, but it faded as he saw that the lawman's wound was troubling him.

'Nope. By my reckoning three horses headed south around the eastern hill.' Mex paused to masticate another mouthful of beans.

The lawman's impatience was manifest and he grunted and stomped until Mex finished his hasty meal, then angry at the Mexican's desire to light a cheroot, hauled himself into the saddle and stared reproachfully at Mex who did precisely what he wanted. The pards grinned at each other as they eventually climbed into their saddles.

For the next hour they rode at an easy pace dictated by the clouds crossing the moon's face. Without the meagre light Mex would never travel far from the general direction of the trail during the times the moon was covered. It was just struggling clear from a thickly banked cloud when Juarez stopped and hissed a warning to the other two who pulled up just behind him. Mallin grew impatient as he failed to hear anything, but Mex sat stock still, confident. Then Mallin heard at the same time as Clint something or somebody moving towards them.

The sound grew until a few minutes later horses and riders came into view around a bluff in the hill.

'Sullivan and the girl,' snarled Mallin, then the still form on the third horse took his attention. 'Looks like he's salivated another *hombre.*'

Matt and Kathy came on. Recognition had been immediate and they felt they had nothing to fear but Mallin's attitude was a shock to them. The lawman's gun was in his hand as he pushed in front of his companions.

'Keep coming you coyote and keep your hands away from that knife of yours or you won't live to get hung.'

The youngsters flashed looks of consternation at one another but Matt did as he was bid and came to within a few feet of the deputy. Clint and Mex pulled around Mallin and took a look at the corpse. There was respect in their eyes when they looked at young Matt.

'I'm taking you back to Portales,' Mallin

183

started, then glowered as Clint butted in savagely.

'Stow the talk, Mallin! The youngster's toting Carlson's corpse. Suppose you let 'em tell their story.'

'Carlson!?' Mallin gulped. 'Sure. Let's hear it.'

Matt told his story simply, minimizing the final fight with Carlson but Kathy filled in all the details. She had to talk to rid her mind of the horror of the last few hours, and anyway, she was proud of her Matt. Mallin peered across at the youngster's bruised face then suddenly he holstered his gun and held out his hand. Matt looked at it doubtfully for a moment then gripped it.

'I'm not going to detain you people any longer,' the lawman said quietly. 'I guess I'll tote all the dead men back and leave you to go about your business.'

He shook hands with the pards and Kathy, then when the horses carrying the corpses had been tethered one to another he turned to go.

'I'd be mighty obliged if you'd let me know how things pan out at the end of your trail,' he said.

'You can rely on that,' Clint replied. 'We'll mail you a full account. I guess it's owing to you for having the good sense to let Sullivan free.'

Mallin kneed his mount and headed away.

The long trail of led horses strung out behind him.

They made Elida in the early hours of the morning, and after stabling their mounts managed to find room in a shambling hotel that had seen better days. The beds were none too soft but the fact went unnoticed. They all slept the moment their heads touched the pillows.

The pardners awoke at sunup and after washing and breakfasting, spent an hour leaning on the handrail along the sidewalk, watching Elida come to life. A stage coach spewed dust as fresh horses brought it from around the back of the Fargo depot. A couple of prairie schooners with a lightning flash painted along their canvas sides grated to a halt outside a hardware store, and outside the office with the sheriff's shingle above it, a neat, clean-shaven little man of about thirty stood eyeing them. There was a star on his vest, and he gave the impression of setting a great deal of store by that star.

'I guess he sees most strangers who pass through his territory,' Clint murmured and Mex paused in the act of lighting a cheroot to nod. They made their way over to the lawman who watched their approach with studied calm.

'Howdye, Sheriff,' Clint said easily. 'The name's Bellamy, Clint Bellamy, and my pard's Mex Juarez.'

The lawman nodded and pointed to the shingle. The pards read: J.S. Rutter. Sheriff of Elida County. 'Well, what's on your minds?' he asked.

'We're trailing a *hombre* who may be dressed in padre's outfit,' Clint replied. 'He was heading for Elida and could have come through anytime within the last day.'

Rutter shook his head decisively. 'Nope, there's been no padre through Elida in a year. Suppose you tell me why you're trailing him anyway.'

'He was with a wagon train of immigrants from way back east,' Mex put in quickly. 'They just want him back. I guess he was a real comfort to 'em.'

Rutter eyed Mex sceptically but the Mexican's expression remained bland and the sheriff shrugged his shoulders.

'Well, if he shows up I'll tell him what you say,' he said levelly. He knew well enough that the pardners were holding something back and made it clear that he was not prepared to dicker without the full facts. There was a moment's silence then the pards turned away and walked up Main Street.

'Reckon we'd have had him on our necks if we'd wised him up,' Mex growled. 'Let's try the livery stable.'

A couple of minutes later they stood watching a whipcord thin oldster unbaling a couple of stooks of straw ready for spreading around the cleaned floor of the large stable. The man looked up.

'You fellers want your broncs?'

'Yeah. We might as well take 'em now,' Clint replied.

The oldster stood aside as Mex and Clint saddled up the four horses. He eyed the pinto and dun gelding appreciatively. 'Couple of good broncs you're forking,' he murmured.

'Yep, we've sure had some good offers for them,' Clint replied. 'A *hombre* who was headed this way a day ahead of us out of Portales was ready to let us set our own price.'

The liveryman raised his eyebrows. 'Horse dealer?' he queried. 'I guess most dealers passing through this territory take a look around my stock.'

'Don't know,' Clint commented. 'Mebbe he did call.' He gave a brief description of Belman in a half-hearted sort of way as he pulled some money out of his money belt.

'That jasper went south on the Roswell stage yesterday morning,' the oldster said. 'Stabled his broncs in the Fargo stable the night before. He had 'em hitched to the back of the stage when he travelled south. Blamed if I know how a *hombre* could favour the inside of a coach instead of forking his cayuse.'

The pards left the livery man and led the animals down Main Street to the hitchrail in front of the hotel. They had been fortunate to find a garrulous livery man. As a breed, livery men were as tight as clams.

'If you get Matt and Kathy I'll see what I can find out in the staging depot,' Clint said and Mex headed for the hotel.

Clint was lucky again. The desk man was busy in the back office and Clint had time to scan the passenger list. Only one man had taken a seat on the Roswell stage and the name was shown as M. Bullen. A couple of minutes went by then a bright-eyed man stepped into the front office and smiled easily.

'Can I help you?' he asked.

'I heard my pard Mose Bullen pulled out on the Roswell run yesterday. Did he book on from Roswell?'

The clerk's eyes strayed to the passenger list that he had been busy on earlier and back to Clint who returned the look with a bland expression.

'Yeah. He booked clear to El Paso.' The clerk paused and looked doubtfully at the tough-looking Texan. 'You thinking of taking the stage?'

Clint shook his head and grinned. 'Nope. I reckon he took the stage to give me the chance to catch up with him before El Paso. I'm sure obliged to you,' he added as he turned to go.

The clerk watched the Texan leave and for a moment his conscience niggled him.

Maybe he had divulged information that was purely Fargo business, but he dismissed the thought. The Texan looked a straight shooter.

Clint joined up with the others in the hotel dining-hall, and he and Mex whiled away the time drinking cups of scalding coffee until Matt and Kathy finished breakfast. If Belman intended riding stage to El Paso they had time to spare. It was a four-day stage run and he was one day in front, but they could do it in just under three days.

They left Elida about three hours after sunup, neither Matt nor Kathy questioning the other two. There was a new air about Matt Sullivan that neither Clint nor Mex failed to notice. The outcome of his brush with Carlson had increased his confidence and he had become very much a man amongst men. The pardners were glad to see his step into manhood, as much for Kathy's sake as Matt's.

During the long run to Roswell they kept to the stage route, the tried and tested trail through the endless run of deep canyons and giddy heights where the land on one side fell away to apparently bottomless depths through forests of ponderosa pine, balsam, poplars, hemlock and maple to the cactus plants, eking out a bare subsistence from the desert at the foot of the mountains. Throughout the long ride when the temperatures ranged from freezing point to sizzling heat, Matt and Kathy kept pace, and all the time maintained a heart-warming cheerfulness.

It was about sundown when they beheld the trail stretching down in a long ribbon to the sparkling waters of the Pecos, and beyond to the huddled buildings of Roswell. They forded the Pecos in the shallows where it spilled over an upthrust of impermeable rock and entered Roswell when the lights were starting to show in saloons and stores. They stayed to rest their mounts and get themselves a meal, then just before midnight, headed south-west towards the Sacramento Mountains. This stage of the journey to Alamagarde was the most difficult and dangerous of the whole ride. The trail wound around an outer ring of the Sacramentos at a fairly even gradient but all the way, one side of the rutted road fell away sheer to the eroded spires of stone far below. The distance from Elida to Alamagarde was only forty miles but it was understandable that the stage crawled this section in a full day's run of twelve hours. The going was safer on horseback but at night-time no relaxation of vigilance was permissible. When the moon showed, the going was easier, but too often the bulk of the mountain masked the moon's light and the pards kept the speed down to safe limits.

At length they stopped for a meal and brief

rest in a deep cavern out of the bitter wind, and they were thankful for the Mexican's foresight in having lumbered the pack-horse with driftwood from the Pecos valley. The fire was welcome and the piping hot coffee a searing pleasure. Refreshed and re-invigorated they pushed on until dawn found them just above the plateau that housed the vast herds of cattle responsible for the town of Alamagarde. When they rode wearily into town the stage coach rolled away from the staging depot, and two horses were tethered to its rear rail.

Clint and Mex exchanged satisfied glances. Belman was within range. They could get close to him anytime they wished. The long night ride however had dimmed the enthusiasm of Matt and Kathy, and as they carried on down Main Street to the livery stable they lolled heavily in their saddles. To the pards' experienced eyes the signs were obvious. For all their spirit the two youngsters were hard put to maintain their morale. The stiff manner in which they slipped to the ground outside the livery stable filled the pards with concern and when Mex led the animals into the livery, Clint piloted Matt and Kathy back up Main Street.

'I guess we can use some chow first then we'll get ourselves some shut-eye for a few hours,' he said briskly. Relief flooded into Kathy's face and Matt managed the first smile for many hours.

Six hours later they quit town towards the snow-capped peaks of the Sacramentos. The mountains appeared to pose a magnificent but terrifying barrier to progress beyond their bulk. Matt stared at them for a time then pushed his mount abreast of the pards.

'Have we got to climb over those mountains?' he asked, pointing to the west.

Mex turned in the saddle and shook his head. 'Nope, I guess not, Matt. This trail runs through the Sacramentos then it's fairly easy down to the Rio Grande and El Paso.'

Satisfied, Matt waited for Kathy and passed on the information. The rest had done wonders for the girl, and her smile as she drew his attention to the beauty of the Sacramentos, set his heart pounding like a steam hammer.

'The only beauty I see right now, Kathy, is your own, and I guess everything else will always be second rate.'

Kathy sobered in tune with his mood and womanlike pushed the conversation on the way she wanted.

'Well then, Matt, this place El Paso, maybe it's pretty big, with a church and all. Maybe we could stay long enough to...' She allowed her words to tail away but the excited gleam in Matt's eyes told her he was in step.

'You – you'll marry me then?' he asked quickly, searching her face hungrily.

'Of course I'll marry you, Matt. I've thought of nothing more since I turned into a woman.'

They rode in utter contentment, secure in the knowledge that they would never part from each other. Up front, Mex and Clint were considering their quarry, Mose Belman.

'Why El Paso?' Clint asked for the tenth time. 'With that much gold he could go anywhere.'

'El Paso might be anywhere as far as Belman's concerned.'

Clint grinned. 'Yeah. I see what you mean, but why not get the thing cut down to size? If I was toting that much gold I'd stash it small.'

They rode in silence for a long time, but there was a very pensive look on the Mexican's face. Clint rolled himself a cigarette and allowed Mex to get on with his thinking.

'I've gotta cousin,' Mex announced after a while and Clint smiled. He had heard plenty about Mex's sisters. Now it seemed he had run out of sisters.

'Juanita, yeah Juanita. She used to stay on our *estancia* with my sisters–' Mex mused. There was a pause while he considered Juanita and Clint gathered the girl had meant a lot to his pard. 'Well, Juanita married Ramon Deloros down in Deloros Valley just

193

about twenty miles south of Ciudad Juarez. I heard her tell of the family church that was pillaged by soldiers returning from the Great Plains back in sixteen hundred. The Deloros, like the Juarez, had settled twenty years earlier into *encomiendas*. The peons had been fervently religious even then.' Mex flashed a glance at Clint to see that he was taking things in. 'It seems the cross that was taken from the church was something mighty special, fashioned in gold with rings of precious stones and a central ruby that was worth a fortune. I remember the church well. Instead of adobe, it had been fashioned out of granite from the Guadalupes, but I remember the empty cradle that had supported the cross and the wrought-iron arm holders still in place. Well, the belief has always been that the cross would be returned. The dying words of the priest after the soldiers had left promised just that. Perhaps that promise is about to be fulfilled.'

'But how would Belman fit in?' Clint asked.

'If he knows the Deloros, then he knows they will pay far more than the face value to have the cross back in place. It's worth the try. If the cross is the wrong one he can cut it and trade it later.' Mex eyed his pard thoughtfully. 'Somehow I've a feeling that cross belongs in Deloros.'

'And how about the folk in the wagon

train?' Clint asked. 'As far as we know it belongs to them and as I see it we're obliged to return it to them.'

Mex pushed his sombrero back and scratched his thick black hair. 'I'm making no plans on account of that hunk of gold, Clint. If that is the Deloros cross then it sure seems to know where it wants to be. Just think, it's crossed the ocean and spent a couple of centuries in Europe and now it's back within a hundred miles of its home. No sir, I'm just going to let things work out.'

Another point from Mex's story had taken Clint's attention. Clint had been to El Paso just once, and remembered the fabulous city of Ciudad Juarez across the other side of the Rio Grande, and now for the first time linked his pard with the powerful family who had created the city.

'Just how far over the border is your *estancia*, Mex?' he asked, and the Mexican flashed him an understanding glance.

'Maybe eight miles but we've got places in the city.'

'And how far removed are you from the Juarez of Ciudad Juarez?'

'In direct line, Clint. One of these days I'll have to settle and take my responsibilities, but not yet. Fortunately my father and his father are in good health. Maybe when the time comes, you'll find enough to interest you in the territory.' Mex did not look at his pard as he replied but Clint knew the sincerity would be there. Then Clint grinned as he wondered which sister would be inveigled into providing the interest.

They relapsed into silence on the long run through the Sacramentos and the pards gave themselves over to the pure enjoyment of the ride, the appreciation of scenes that could be matched in very few places. They passed a remount depot, and an hour later had a meal beside an ice-cold rivulet of water that had cut its course down from the snowline. Then when the sun shed its slanting rays over the evening sky, they had their first glimpse of the stage coach since Alamagarde. Belman was no more than four miles away and could be taken as and when they pleased.

It was after about two hours of darkness that Mex pulled his pinto to a halt. Clint reined in and the other two pulled in close behind him.

'I'm taking a short route to Deloros just in case Belman decides to give El Paso a miss. Just trail him, Clint. Let him go where he wants. If he doesn't show up in Deloros in a day after I arrive I'll pick up your trail in El Paso.'

Such was their understanding that Clint did no more than grunt assent, then with the briefest of hand-clasps, Mex faded into the night and Clint urged Matt and Kathy in the wake of the stage coach. As they rode he told them the story of the church of Deloros as Mex had said it, and the possibility that the cross of Mournaghee and the cross of Deloros were one and the same, went some way to consoling them as they realized they would not be lingering in El Paso.

The moon was slow in spilling its eerie light over the trail, but when it finally showed the stage breasting a rise a mile or so ahead, Clint stopped and grunted in annoyance. The led horses were gone. Belman had done just what Mex had thought he might do. Angrily, Clint turned his attention to the trail. Belman had covered his tracks well and the Texan had to be content in taking a thinly marked trail that ran across the mountain to the south. He saw no sign of Belman, and an hour later Matt observed maybe Belman had decided he could reach El Paso a lot faster on horseback. Then a silhouette against the skyline a few miles later reassured Clint, and he settled down to the hunt.

Belman waited impatiently in the oven-like interior of the stage coach. Being cooped up was plain hell to him, but he had reasoned he was far less conspicuous travelling by stage than on horse-back, and he was well satisfied to have arrived thus far without trouble.

Every now and again he stuck his head out

of the coach and quartered the terrain, using a pair of field glasses he had acquired on the east coast. Time and again he saw nothing, then just before sunset he saw them. Shading the glasses to prevent any reflection, he stared in disbelief at the four riders. 'Bellamy and Juarez,' he muttered. Matt and Kathy he dismissed without thought. These men were like leeches and there was only one way to deal with them, but first he would trade in the cross. His plans were already made, and he knew just where he would be leaving the stage for the short cut to Deloros.

With the coming of night, Belman stood staring hard into the gloom for the break in the left-hand face of the mountain that opened into the trail he remembered to the tree bridge across the Rio Grande just twenty miles south of El Paso, and no more than five miles from the church of Deloros. Such was his impatience that he seemed to have been standing in the swaying, creaking coach for all eternity, yet it was no more than ninety minutes before his keen eyes picked up contours in the rock wall that stirred his memory. They reached the top of a long grade, and Belman drew a deep satisfied breath.

'Haul 'em in, driver!' he yelled. 'This'll do!'

The driver pulled back at the leaders and applied the brake, bringing the coach to a stop before the down gradient made itself felt. He climbed down stiff-legged, eyeing Belman doubtfully. He was carrying registered packages from places up the line as far as Santa Fe, and for once he had no guard. He was no slouch with a gun but something about Belman suggested he was outclassed. When his passenger moved around the coach to unhitch the horses the driver exhaled heavily with relief.

'Just pass down that box of mine and you can be on your way.'

Belman's words stirred the driver, who climbed up and tried handing down the box Belman had obtained in Portales. The weight did not match the appearance of the thin cheap wood and he had to climb on top of the coach and handle it with a lot more strength and determination.

His passenger grunted his thanks and with some skill, fastened the box to the back of his pack-horse so that it would ride safely. The driver bit back the question why his passenger elected to get off in the middle of nowhere, and returning to the driving seat released the brake, sending the coach rumbling into the night. A minute later Belman swung into the saddle and headed off trail across the face of the mountain.

The nearness of Bellamy and Juarez kept niggling him as he picked his way through the blanket-like blackness of night, but he reasoned that he would gain sufficient lead before they discovered he had parted company with the stage, and there should be no hitch in his plans. No matter how much he persuaded himself there was no cause for concern, the nagging memory of the two men as seen through the field glasses persisted. They had looked so relaxed and assured, and a niggling presentiment deepened with every mile he covered.

With the moon clear of the hills, Belman travelled with the care of the born night traveller, moving in the shadows of trees and rocks that stood like calcified sentinels. Once, when rounding a hill, he felt almost naked as he was silhouetted against the skyline, and he cursed roundly as he saw tiny black figures moving in front of an escarpment of pure white limestone. He passed beyond the bluff and brought back to mind what he had seen: three riders and a led horse. So either Bellamy or Juarez had followed the route to El Paso. A slow smile spread over Belman's features. The combination of Bellamy and Juarez was cause enough for concern, but one or the other should not present difficulties.

The trail ran true, and when the mist broke free of the Rio Grande and crawled up the mountain, he saw the massive sections of sequoia that spanned the towering gorge above the fast-running river. He spared little thought for the hundreds of peons who had struggled to bridge the gorge at its narrowest point a century earlier, and even less on the durability of the tree. His main concern was the other side of the river that was Mexico, and the five miles further on that was Deloros and untold wealth.

Another trail from the mountains converged near the bridge, but Belman thought nothing of the hoof-prints that showed coming off the trail. He coaxed his mount over, and then sent the animal at speed towards the wide valley indicated by two round hills rising out of the undulating grassland. Glancing behind, he saw three riders etched on the skyline on a shoulder of the mountain he had descended and he laughed aloud in his knowledge that they had lost ground. He sobered, presenting a more nonchalant demeanour as he came up to the first large bunch of cattle between him and the valley of Deloros. A couple of hot-eyed *vaqueros* watched him suspiciously and he saw one frame the word 'Gringo' with sneering lips, but he ignored them and swept on.

The hills loomed closer as his long striding horse responded to the demand for speed, until at last, Belman caught the first glimpse of the granite dome of the church of St Theresa towering above the adobe town buildings. With eyes agleam with satisfaction, he joined the rutted road that entered through a thick adobe wall bordering the

201

town, and a few minutes later rode slowly through the gateway.

It seemed to Belman that every last man and woman was gathered in the market-place of Deloros; peons, *vaqueros*, traders. All stopped whatever they were doing to watch his progress down the street. Some stood in absolute silence, but others closed in behind him and followed quietly. Belman's scalp started to itch as he rode deeper into the town, but as he neared the turning that led to the church, the following crowd halted and he breathed easier. Keeping to the middle of the roadway he took the turning and stared towards the entrance to the church precincts.

For a moment he forgot the silent crowd. The white dusty road stretched ahead, the last stretch, just a hundred yards before he would enjoy the cool interior of the church and name his own price for the cross. Gringo he might be, but how the crowd would change when they saw the treasure he had brought them. Fifty yards and the sweat stood out on Belman's face as his thoughts excited him, then he pulled his mount in and stared in utter amazement at the slim figure of a man who had emerged from behind a gate pillar to stand four-square, a few yards away from the church gate.

'Juarez!' The name escaped from Belman's lips in a sibilant hiss.

'Just climb down, Belman. You've come to

the end of the trail.' Mex spoke quietly, but his words seemed to hang in the air, so quiet had the town of Deloros become.

Belman shook his head in disbelief, then slowly he dropped out of the saddle. The shock had completely robbed him of his poise. Not only had the greaser outsmarted him but his real name was known to the man also. He pulled himself together with an effort. It was still possible to salvage everything. He had never met a faster gunslinger yet, and for all the Mexican's *élan* and calm he reckoned he should have the edge. He moved away from the horses and when he looked again at Mex his manner was easy.

'If you've finished talking I'm ready.' As Belman spoke, he dropped into a crouch and the Mexican's lips parted in a grin.

It seemed as though an age went by with the adversaries staring at each other through slitted eyes, and the crowd holding their breath in suspense, yet it was no more than five seconds before the guns roared. Belman's gun went off as his fingers convulsed in a reflex action after the bullet from Mex Juarez' smoking gun entered his heart, and the shot ploughed up dust just a couple of feet in front of his teetering body.

For a few seconds Belman staggered crazily, then he clutched at the straps keeping the load in place on the pack-horse. He hung on for a moment, then down he went, dragging the load down upon him. The thin boxwood split and shattered, and the cross of Deloros gleamed in the harsh sunlight across Belman's body.

Half-an-hour later Clint, Matt and Kathy rode through the gate of Deloros to be welcomed by a tumultuous roar of approval from crowds lining the sidewalks. On all sides excited Mexicans gesticulated wildly and others with money to burn fired shots into the air. Clint sat his dun gelding with a slow grin on his face but Matt and Kathy were bewildered by it all. They clasped hands for reassurance and the cheering increased. All Mexicans have a special feeling for young lovers.

There was only one route open to the riders. The crowd blocked every other turn and at last the cavalcade turned into the road leading to the church. In front of the gates a group of people stood talking animatedly. In the middle of the group was Mex, his white teeth gleaming in a smile, black eyes shining with excitement. He stepped away from the group to welcome the newcomers.

Clint slid out of the saddle and the other two followed suit, Mex handing Kathy down. The group of people came forward and Mex made the introductions. The Deloros family was there in strength, Carlos, Manuel, Cristo and Ramon, the tall dignified young head of the family. Juanita, Ramon's wife, dazzlingly beautiful and possessed of poise born of centuries of culture. Clint could see the likeness between her and his pard. The padre was there, benign yet flushed with the excitement of the moment.

'It is all arranged,' Mex said, more to Matt and Kathy than to Clint. 'The cross is back in its rightful place. Your people were looking for a place to settle and a place to worship. Well, the valley of Deloros welcomes you, and as your religion is their religion, you can share this church with the Deloros. Clint and I will bring the wagon train to the valley.'

There were tears in Kathy's eyes as the words brought the knowledge of security, and a big smile of contentment spread over Matt's face. Juanita came forward to Kathy's side and embraced her in real womanly welcome.

'There's one thing the people of Deloros would like,' Mex said. 'That's a special service, something to celebrate the return of the cross.' He looked from Matt to Kathy with kindly eyes. 'Maybe a wedding,' he added.

Matt's hand was entwined with Kathy's and he turned to her, the question in his eyes. The girl nodded, her eyes brimming with tears of happiness.

In a matter of minutes the crowds had vanished. Matt had been borne away by Ramon and his brothers whilst Kathy departed amidst a throng of women with Juanita. The people of Deloros had gone to put on their celebration dress. Just Clint and Mex stood at the door of the church of Deloros, staring down the long aisle to where the cross reflected the shafts of light coming through the chancel windows.

'I reckoned that left to itself, that hunk of gold would work things out,' Mex muttered, and Clint, struck by its beauty, could only nod his agreement.

The publishers hope that this book has given you enjoyable reading. Large Print Books are especially designed to be as easy to see and hold as possible. If you wish a complete list of our books please ask at your local library or write directly to:

The Golden West Large Print Books
Magna House, Long Preston,
Skipton, North Yorkshire.
BD23 4ND

This Large Print Book, for people
who cannot read normal print,
is published under the auspices of

THE ULVERSCROFT FOUNDATION